CORONAVIRUS: A NOVEL

MARGARET NYHON

Willow Press

CONTENTS

Published by Willow Press

Author contact: margaretf@hotmail.co.nz

A catalogue record for this book is available from the National Library of New Zealand.

ISBN 9780473581787 (paperback)

ISBN 9780473581794 (EPUB)

'I want to say to my sisters and brothers
Keep the faith when the storm flies
And the wind blows'
Keep the faith as the virus spreads
And the fires burn
Keep the faith and make our planet safe
And love and care for each other
Keep the faith we need it now
more
than
Ever!

1

THE LABORATORY

THE PHARMACEUTICAL LABORATORY in Xihun had been in full production and now that the secret chemical was completed and locked away in the vault, everyone's life was in order once again and they were back at their usual jobs. It had been an interruption for all the workers, and no-one knew what they had helped to manufacture as it was top secret. Only the laboratory staff and the scientists knew; the workers had been kept in the dark. No-one in the factory asked questions, as they were paid to work and that's what they did; that's just how things were. It was not often they were asked to perform unusual tasks, but they didn't dare ask for fear of losing their jobs. Occasionally they were allowed to visit the nursery where the animals were kept in cages, as they were experimental specimens, but still no questions!

There was a big turnover of animal caretakers; no-one seemed to last long, as often vacancies were advertised in the paper. Chen saw an advertisement so he decided to apply. There didn't seem to be any special criteria for this position, and no previous experience was required. He was asked about his marital status and whether he had children and was close to his family, which he thought was strange. Did he mind traveling into the wilds to capture the odd animal when needed? This he thought sounded exciting and appealing. A vehicle was provided for transport when capturing the animals.

He needed money to help out his parents as jobs weren't that easy to come by. He lived in a tiny apartment with his new wife just as hundreds of other families did, in highly condensed neighbourhoods, as was the norm for peasants. His wife was pleased he had a job with a large company, although he couldn't tell her much about his work as all employees had to sign a letter of confidentiality, and no talk from the workplace was to be repeated outside.

The outline of his job was not very clear at first, but as he was a keen worker, he would do his best to please everyone. For the first couple of days, he watered and fed the animals and cleaned their cages. All the manure was shovelled into big bins in a lined cupboard, which he was pleased had a heavy door, as the smell was most unpleasant. He did wonder why the animals were there as it was dark and dingy and wondered what part they played in the laboratory, as it was not a nice environment for them to be kept in. He wasn't allowed to venture past the double doors marked 'Private' as his position only allowed him entry to the nursery. Chen likened his workplace to a secret service organisation, but as with all the other workers he needed the money, so asked no questions.

On his third day, as he cycled into work a truck was waiting and a man yelled to him, "Bring your lunch. We are off into the wilds today." Chen grabbed his lunch and climbed into the vehicle. There was very little conversation between the two men as they drove out of the city. He did wonder what they were going to catch as he had noticed cages on the deck of the truck. Several hours later they drove off the main highway and entered a narrow gravelled side-road. As they progressed it narrowed until it was no more than a track, overgrown with trees and bushes. The further they went the more overgrown it became. Suddenly the vehicle came to an abrupt stop and the driver announced, "We are here!" On alighting he was told to grab a couple of cages, so they both trudged through the undergrowth loaded up, until they came upon a partial clearing where they put the cages down and rested for a moment. It was only then that Chen realised there was food wired to the cages.

His workmate, who he understood was called Tan, seemed to be familiar with what was happening. He went over to a cluster of tall trees where a ladder was attached to a trunk, and as he readied himself to climb the ladder he called to Chen, "Bring over a small cage and wait until I fetch this one down." Chen did as he was told and stood beneath the ladder wating for further instructions. He watched as Tan reached up into the branches and lifted down a cage that had bats inside. They were not happy with being disturbed so put on a right old performance, flapping around in the cage. Down the ladder he came and handed Chen the full cage in exchange for an empty one. He was a little frightened and bewildered as there were no bats in his nursery, and he wondered why they were bringing these ones back, and who was going to look after them. He didn't particularly like these animals; their odour was anything but pleasant. Tan went back up the ladder and disappeared among the branches. Only a few minutes passed before he emerged with another full cage, so the same sequence was repeated.

The two men trudged back to the vehicle with the full cages and placed them under a tarpaulin that lay on the truck deck. They then proceeded to eat their lunch before retracing their steps back into the wilds. This time they picked up the other empty cages and headed in a totally different direction until they came across a lake. Chen followed Tan as he knew where he was heading. They walked around the perimeter of the wetlands to where another couple of cages were partially hidden. He was surprised to find several salamanders huddled together in each cage. Tan picked them up and handed them to Chen who knew they weren't as fearful as they looked, as they didn't have claws. He had several back at the nursery. Tan took a little box out of his pocket and put two eggs in each empty cage, which he placed in the same position. "We are all done here. Let's take these creatures back to the vehicle," he told Chen.

As they were homeward bound Chen plucked up enough courage to ask Tan why the last caretaker had left the company. "He just disappeared, and no-one knows what happened to him. He didn't come home from work one day so his family never knew what happened!" This was thought-provoking stuff for Chen. Why didn't anyone know what had happened to their workmate? Did they not care? "Does this happen often?" he asked. Tan was hesitant before giving a reply. "There are certain things that go on in the company that there doesn't seem to be answers to, but we all need our jobs so turn a blind eye, but yes, things do happen." There the subject came to a close as Tan hummed away to himself.

On their arrival back at company headquarters Tan told Chen to take the salamanders to the nursery. "What about the bats?" he asked. "They are coming with me," was the answer he received in a tone that told him not to pry further. He settled the salamanders in their rightful places on the shelves then proceeded to feed the rest of his charges. The rats were hungry so made their presence felt, but the mice were more passive as they still had grain left in their troughs from the day before. Now it was time to gather all the day's droppings and carry them to the bins, which were hidden in the cupboard. Each day the stench nearly made him dry-retch. When were the bins going to be emptied and who was going to do it? He had been there a week now and they were nearly full. Tomorrow was Saturday and he only worked the morning so hopefully something would be done by then. As he locked up, Chen thought back over his day and there seemed to be a lot of questions unanswered, but he could not discuss anything outside the workplace. He wished he could talk to his father to see what he thought, as he was a very wise man.

The next morning, when Chen arrived at work, he was surprised to see two young men wheel the waste bins out the back door and empty them into a large drain. But where does the drain go, he wondered, surely not under the building, as the marketplace was next door where fresh food was sold along with live animals. Even cooked and raw food sat next to each other on open shelves alongside live animals stacked in cages. This was where he himself shopped, as did most of the apartment dwellers, as it was close to where they lived. It catered for everyone.

"How often do you empty the bins?" asked Chen. "We do them on a Saturday, although this is only our second time. The last two guys just disappeared; we are new." What did he mean, they just disappeared? How did they just disappear? No-one just disappears, thought Chen. "Had they worked for the company long?" Chen asked. "Apparently the smell puts them off so they don't come back; no-one lasts long." This explanation put Chen's mind at rest, and perhaps 'disappeared' wasn't the right word to be using. He went inside and gave the animals a double dose of food as they would not be fed again until Monday when he came back to work.

Another week had passed and it was Saturday once again. Chen and Tan had been to the wilds through the week and brought back another four cages of salamanders and bats. This time one cage of bats came to the nursery, which was unusual. He had nowhere to put them so sat them on the floor in the meantime, until he made another shelf.

Today there were two new guys emptying the 'poo-bins' and a stray dog was accompanying them. "Are you new here?" enquired Chen. "Where are the other guys?" "We were asked to report for duty today, don't know about anyone else." Chen stood and scratched his head: what is going on? And just at that moment the silence was broken by a yelp. Chen tore inside to find the dog had killed one of the bats in the cage, but not without a fight as the dog had an open wound on his nose, thus the yelping. "Get that dog out. Domestic pets are not allowed to mix with wild animals," he yelled to the lads. With this one of the lads grabbed the dog and tied him up to one of their bicycles. He was still whimpering as he was in pain. Chen carried on and fed the animals and by the time he managed to get back to remove the dead bat, a snake had slithered across the floor through the wire cage and was devouring it.

When the lads finished, it was also Chen's knock-off time so he followed the lads and their dog next door to the market. It was not uncommon to see stray mangy dogs hanging around the market. That was just how life was lived and in fact it was a breeding ground for diseases, as rats and mice also hung out here. There was no running water, and feathers from the caged birds who were flapping in fright landed on cooked and raw food alike. But this did not deter the locals; it was a different story for overseas visitors, however. Very few tourists bought food as they had been warned against the non-cleanliness of these places. They wandered through with horror on their faces and in utter disgust. It was an education for them to see how the poorer people lived in these highly populated areas.

The locals seemed happy and were very polite, but their means of earning enough money to buy food often forced them to take on whatever jobs were available, as had happened to Chen. His job was not his choice of work, but as the saying goes 'beggars can't be choosers'. Life had to go on and food had to be paid for, therefore any sort of work was work, after all was said and done!

On Monday Chen had to let management know that there had been a mishap in the nursery, and this upset him: was he going to lose his job? His wife would not be happy, nor would his parents. He stood in front of the big desk and explained what had happened. He was shouted at, as the rule was no domestic pets were allowed to come in contact with the wild animals. He was thankful that this was all the punishment he received; he still had his job.

The following Saturday morning the same two lads arrived with their dog, which Chen told them to tie well away from the nursery. They went about their job emptying and cleaning the smelly poo-bins into the drain beside the market. Chen hadn't realised before he came to work at his job how unsanitary the environment was surrounding the marketplace. He had just accepted the market, as this was where he had come to do his shopping for the past twenty years.

In his nursery he had to breed mice to feed the snakes and now the bats. Frogs also had to be brought to feed the bats. In the wetlands the bats ate flying insects such as mosquitos and midges, frogs and mice along with plants, but now their diet would change. For so many different species to be kept in captivity together was fraught with danger. Chen didn't fully understand what was happening, as each day animals were taken away by the laboratory assistants for short periods of time, then returned. Then when they were finished with, they were taken to the market and sold. So, what were people eating, what tests had been carried out on these animals before going to the market? Chen was just happy to have a job, and he wasn't savvy enough to weigh up the consequences of all the happenings going on around him. He wasn't an educated man, just a pheasant who worked to provide for his wife and elderly parents.

2

CONSEQUENCES!

ONE DAY when Chen came home from work, he found his wife unconscious on their bed. She hadn't been well for a week, but it was thought to be a flu. He tried to wake her to no avail, so he cycled around to his parents' house. They both came back with him, but it was too late – she had passed away. They bent down and kissed her, as they said their final farewells. Chen was devastated as he had not had time to say goodbye; now it would never be heard. Just as well he had a job to take his mind away from his grief. He decided to give up his flat and move back in with his parents, so he could care for them. But it wasn't long before his mother became sick, and was diagnosed with pneumonia, from which she never recovered. Chen and his father battled on in their home. Times were sad, but they drew comfort from each other.

Nothing much changed in Chen's workplace apart from the high turnover of the casual poo-bin lads. It was concerning that so many young lads just disappeared and never came back. It was a well-paid job because it was not a pleasant one; in fact it was enough to keep a family for a week. These thoughts came and went. Then one day his father fell ill with the same problem his mother suffered, a chest infection, and the inevitable happened. Now Chen had no-one, and he drifted into deep depression, feeling that his life had come to an end. Why had he lost all those close to him? But he was not alone in this, as much of the neighbourhood was suffering from the same debilitating chest infections. It was common talk in the marketplace where everyone shopped that the movement of people in a confined area was a perfect place for diseases to pass from one person to the next.

Soups of all varieties were made from anything, from snakes to bats, and purchased every day and ladled into bowls for a quick, cheap snack. Affordability played a big part in what people ate. There was such a variety of food: fresh, cooked, raw and rotten lay alongside the livestock – chickens, salamanders, bats, snakes, cats and dogs. Often the heads would be chopped off the chickens and ducks and blood spurted everywhere, but life went on and so did mysterious diseases that weren't yet recognised.

Chen often wondered what was behind the closed doors at work marked 'Private'. He often saw men in white suits coming and going carrying trays of glass vials. They wore masks and gloves, and he wondered whether they were in fact chemists, not lab technicians; and what were they making? The thought of him losing his job prevented him from asking questions, and he was also frightened of those higher up in the hierarchy, as they never spoke with their workers.

One day Chen bought a newspaper, as he heard through work that unrest was brewing with a neighbouring state. He didn't understand the politics of the two countries, so thought he would read and try to take in why this was happening. He didn't want to appear empty-headed among his fellow workers. He never contributed much to their conversations, so perhaps by reading the paper he could at least keep up with them, or even just understand what they were talking about. He was not a man of the world.

There was another article that drew his attention. Many elderly people were dying with respiratory problems, exactly what happened to his wife and parents. Was there a flu going around causing these deaths? Were there more than the normal amount of people getting sick? Apparently so – but why? He pondered over this as he had thought his family died of a flu, but was there another reason? Then he spotted a second article of interest. Many young men from their area were missing and families were asking for help to find them. Why would they just go missing: was missing the same as disappearing? His mind immediately turned to the young lads that came and went at his work, the ones emptying the poo-bins on a Saturday. Could these be the ones they were asking about? How could he find out? There was an address to make contact if anyone could offer any information on their whereabouts. Chen decided to find out, so on Sunday, his day off, he would make contact.

Today was Sunday, so Chen was on his way to meet the persons enquiring about their son. The address wasn't far from where he lived. It was a housing block, nineteen storeys high with hundreds of flats, and was in a poverty-stricken area, but there were plenty of these scattered throughout the city, given that there were millions of people living in a densely populated city. Once he found the right flat, he knocked and waited. An elderly man opened the door and asked, "Are you here about our son?" Chen asked if he could come in, as he may be able to help. They went inside where a frail-looking old lady was wrapped up in a rug sitting in a chair. "Someone is here to talk about our son," he told her. "What do you know?" the man asked. Chen didn't know where to start. "Where did your son last work?" "He worked on a Saturday for a large pharmaceutical company and was well paid. He wasn't allowed to tell us anything about his work, but Liu and his friend worked together, then they both went missing. It is breaking our hearts; we want our son back," he sobbed. Chen's heart felt heavy. Here were two boys that probably worked with him; it certainly sounded like the company he worked for. "There is a photo of Liu and his dog," pointed out the elderly man. Chen recognised the dog immediately. "Where is the dog now?" He told Chen it had a bad gash on its nose that never healed, and it had died. This sealed his suspicion. This boy had worked with him, and he remembered the day the dog had killed the bat. "Can you tell me anything that may have happened at his work?" he asked. "He came home one day with a mark on his arm where he had been given an injection, he didn't know what for, do you? Then the next day he never came back and we have not seen him since. His friend's parents were suffering just like us, until they both died of pneumonia, which is what my wife has." Chen looked across at the dear old soul who managed a faint smile and knew in his heart that she wasn't going to be here much longer. All he could do was give her a last glimmer of hope. "I know your son. I met him and his friend, but I don't know what has happened to them. Leave it with me and I will try to find out some news for you soon. Do you know of any other parents whose sons have gone missing?" "Yes," the man replied, "that's why we called a meeting. We are concerned and we need to know what is happening to our sons."

Back at home that night Chen was overwhelmed with grief for the families whose sons had gone missing. He was sensing foul play within his company, but why did they inject the boys and where were they now? No wonder there was such a high turnover in the Saturday workers. Were they being used as guinea pigs for something sinister? He knew that if this information left his lips he would be in danger, so silent he would remain. He could tell no-one. This was when he missed his father: he would know what to do!

3

THE MISSING LADS

CHEN DIDN'T KNOW where to start, and he was very mindful of the consequences awaiting him if the company got a whiff of what he had uncovered. He kept his eyes out for any news in the papers hoping he could find clues, but none surfaced. He did, however, read a warning to heads of other countries not to interfere with China's politics or there would be repercussions. What was meant by that? Was there a clue in this threat? If there was, he didn't pick up on it.

He continued with his work at the nursery caring for the animals, but his spirit was broken and he couldn't understand what had happened to the boys who emptied the poo-bins. One thing he had noticed was that the workers' cycle park was not nearly as full as it had been. There seemed to be fewer and fewer workers turning up for work, and even the carpark had many empty spaces. Was the company putting off staff? As he prepared for work on Saturday morning, he hoped the same lads would be back, as this was their third week. In fact he really liked them as they had started to open up to him, and at last he felt he had made some friends. He was surprised to see they had brought a girl with them. "This is my sister Jia Li," said one of the boys. "You wait outside until we are finished," he told her. It wasn't long before a shower of rain approached so Chen asked her to come into the nursery. She was surprised at how many animals were kept in such a small area; in fact, she was saddened by this. "Why are these animals here?" she asked. Before Chen realised, he had told her they were used in the laboratory. Now he had broken his loyalty to the company, and it was too late to backtrack. "Please don't tell anybody what I told you," he begged. She acknowledged his request: "It is safe with me." She told Chen she had just been made redundant and was now at home looking after their elderly parents who were poorly; in fact they were both suffering from chest problems.

Just as the boys were finishing for the morning, they were asked to come to the laboratory so Chen stayed behind and talked with Jia Li. He felt at ease with her; she was the only female he had contact with since losing his wife. He felt strange, and a warm feeling came over him, one he hadn't felt for a long time, but why was this as they were complete strangers?

The boys emerged from the building an hour later to pick-up Jia Li. "We have just been given an injection against the flu; we have to report back at the lab in the morning." With this, they all said their goodbyes. Chen decided to go and visit the elderly couple whose son had disappeared. He couldn't tell them much, but he wanted to let them know he was still working on it. When he arrived at the flat, he was shocked to find it all boarded up. He called out, but there was no reply. A neighbour came out and told him they had both died from pneumonia and weren't found for several days. "They have closed the flat off until it is fumigated," he was told.

Chen closed his eyes and wept into his hands. Such sadness this family had suffered; they must have died of broken hearts not knowing what had happened to their son. The tears kept flowing; he lost control of his emotions. When were people going to stop suffering, he wondered? He made his way back to his dwelling – that was all it could be called – but he was grateful not to have to pay rent. His parents had worked hard and managed to own their own place, humble as it was, but it was now his home. He went straight to bed and cuddled up to his pillow, feeling sad and heartbroken for the deceased family and the suffering they had gone through.

Today was Sunday, Chen's day off, so he decided to busy himself with some repairs to his home. It would take his mind off the sadness that surrounded him. Every now and again an image of Jia Li appeared. This he could not understand, as she was a total stranger, but there was something about her that brought a warmth to him. He worked hard all day and before he realised it darkness was descending, so the day had passed quickly. Tomorrow he would be back caring for the animals.

When Chen arrived at work the next day, Jia Li was

waiting for him and his heart skipped a beat. "Chen, I am so worried I didn't know who to talk to," she was sobbing. "Yesterday I walked to the laboratory with my brother and his friend, and while I was waiting, I saw both of them wearing backpacks and being put into a van. It then drove off. I waited all day, but they never came back. What do you think has happened to them?" Chen's heart froze upon hearing this. Were these boys now classed as missing? Had they joined the rest? What was he going to tell Jia Li? She was so upset he couldn't hurt her any more. "Perhaps they were taken to work elsewhere. Let's wait for a few days and see if they return," he said calmly, but inwardly he was fearful: would they ever be seen again? Jia Li took his hand and thanked him, and that warm feeling was there once again.

All week Chen worried for the safety of the two boys. What was going to happen on Saturday? Would two new lads arrive to empty the 'poo-bins'? But on Friday something unexpected happened. Two laboratory assistants arrived to tell Chen the animals were all going to be taken to the market to be sold. He would no longer be needed, his job would finish on Saturday when he had cleaned and emptied the 'bins', as the company was closing down. Suddenly everything started falling into place, the half-empty carparks and cycle storage; why hadn't he realised this? Shock took over. What about Jia Li's brother? Had she heard from him? If not, what then? Now that the company was closing, who was responsible for the missing boys?

Today as Chen cycled into the company's yard for the

last time, Jia Li was there waiting for him. As he greeted her, he noticed her eyes were red and swollen; she had been crying. "Has your brother come back?" he asked. She couldn't hold it together any longer and burst into tears. "My mother and father have both died of pneumonia and my brother is still missing. I don't know what to do. I have to leave the flat at the end of the month because I can't afford the rent. I just want to die." "Don't say that, Jia Li. Come and stay with me. We will work together to see if we can find your brother." He reached out and took her in his arms hoping to comfort her. God knows she needed it, she was a total mess, as there was no-one left in her family. He hadn't told her this was his last day; she didn't need any more bad news. "Come here at the end of my workday and I will take you to my place." She thanked him and left the yard.

He had never experienced such a long drawn-out day. The animals were taken from the nursery to the market, so all that was left for him to do was the cleaning-up and the emptying of the poo-bins. Secretly he was happy his job had finished and all his ties with the company finished here today. He was feeling a little afraid as to what might happen to him if he stayed on. His trust in the company had vanished, along with the missing boys. This left him free to start delving into the company's laboratory work to find out all he could on the lads' disappearances. As he left the nursery for the last time, Jia Li was waiting for him. She was carrying a small overnight bag. Together they walked towards Chen's house, and he was happy he had spent Sunday doing housework, not for a moment thinking he would be having a guest.

That night Jia Li slept in Chen's parents' bedroom. She went to bed early as she was still suffering from the loss of her parents; her tears fell endlessly, she had no control over them, they did what they needed or wanted to do. And she still had to deal with her missing brother!

Today being Sunday, Chen walked to the shop to buy a weekend paper to see if there was any news on the missing boys. Jia Li was still asleep so he didn't disturb her. When he walked through the shop door it was crowded and people were yelling at each other and waving the paper in their hands. He wondered what all the fuss was about, but it didn't take long for him to find out as the headlines were there, bold and clear … 'Pandemic sweeps the world'. He quickly read what followed and was shocked to read the source of the virus was thought to been the market, next to his workplace. Many people in the city had died, and they now knew the deaths from pneumonia were caused by a rapidly spreading coronavirus. Tears welled up in his eyes. Was that what killed his wife and parents along with Jia Li's parents? It was killing many elderly people. As he continued reading, it revealed the cause was thought to be a virus passed by bats to humans. But people had been sick months earlier, so why had it taken so long, in fact three months, to be made public? Was this a cover-up? In February 2019 the fate of a Chinese researcher, believed to be the world's first Covid-19 patient, remained a mystery. Chen felt sick right down in the pit of his stomach. What was going to happen now?

The whole world was in a tailspin and no-one knew how to handle this virus, which now had the whole world in its grasp! To think it started here in his home city, in the marketplace where he did all his shopping. Chen's mind went into overdrive trying to make sense of all that was happening. Did his workplace shut down because the workers were sick or, worse, had they died? Why weren't they told? Was the laboratory hiding things from the outside world? As he thought back over things he wondered if this was a conspiracy: what was being stored in the vault, and why were the Saturday boys vaccinated when no-one else was? So many questions were spinning around in his mind, but he had to find answers! Then he remembered that Jia Li was home on her own, so he left the shop and hurried back to be with her.

He wondered what her take on this would be. Once they had finished breakfast Chen asked Jia Li to sit down as she had a right to know what was happening. He read out what was in the paper and watched for her reaction. He could almost read her mind as he saw the tears bubbling up in her eyes. "Did we lose our parents to the virus?" she asked. Chen nodded, then reached over and took her hand. There was no response, as she was devoid of any feelings now that the truth was out. He sat in silence, giving her time to absorb what she had just been told. She stood up and reached out to Chen. She needed to be comforted as all had been taken from her, her body felt empty and sad, how was she ever going to recover? He held her in his arms, and his body felt relaxed: here were two people alone together and he hoped they could find solace in each other. Tears slipped down his face, but he didn't know whether they were of joy or sadness, but he was not afraid to let his emotions override him at this moment in time. It just seemed right!

Once Jai Li realised where she was, she apologised for her forwardness, but this was far from a normal situation; it was almost a crisis moment, where true feelings were being expressed. "Don't apologise, Jai Li. We need each other, we have no-one else, and together we can become strong again. There will always be moments of sadness but there can also be times of happiness; let us share both." These words echoed in her mind, and she felt safe and comforted by his kind words, as she had never been spoken to like this before. Was she warming towards him amid all her sadness? Later in the day Jia Li decided to go home to her parents' house to see if there was any news on her missing brother. Chen asked if she needed company, but she wanted to do it on her own, so they said their goodbyes. "I'll come back in a couple of days after I have sorted things out," she called to him. He watched with a heavy heart as she walked away.

The next morning Chen decided to cycle down to his old workplace just to see how he felt and if anyone else was there, then he could start asking questions. As he grew near, he saw the company's building and the market all cordoned off with signs on the fence stating, 'Danger Zone'. Guards were surrounding the area. He approached one of them and asked, "Why is this area closed down?

What happened to the pharmaceutical company?" not letting on it was his old workplace. "I cannot tell you much. All I know is that the virus started in this area, and that is why it is closed off." "Were many of the workers at the company affected with the virus?" he desperately wanted to know. The answer came back, "From what I am told most of them have died because of its close proximity to the market." Poor Chen, he felt sick on hearing this, as it was not what he wanted to hear. Was he going to be next? Was he in fact a carrier and is this why his parents died? So many horrible thoughts began swirling around in his head, bringing back that sickening feeling. But why did Jia Li's parents die? Then he remembered her brother worked for the company. Was there a link between the laboratory and the animals? He would keep his ears open for any clues. Were the deaths of his workmates in fact linked to the laboratory, not the market? Where to from here? Questions were starting to mount up, but there had to be answers.

Jia Li was at her parents' flat sorting out their personal belongings when she looked out the window and spotted the postman stopping at the post boxes near the foyer. She rushed down the stairs hoping there was a letter for her parents. On opening her mailbox there was a single letter addressed to her parents. Immediately she recognised the untidy handwriting … it was from her brother. She tore the letter open, anxious to find out where he was, not noticing it had been posted from overseas. It read: 'Dear family, I am very sick and this is why I am writing. After getting on the plane to America I fell ill and wondered if it was due to the injection. I am laid up in a hotel. The doctor has been and apparently I have pneumonia, a very bad bout and am worried that I won't get to the tourist places the company wanted me to visit. I am not meant to be in touch with anyone for a month, but I am worried about my health. My friend was sent to France. I hope he is okay. If I don't make it home, please remember me. Love Quan.' Jia Li clutched the letter tightly to her chest and began to cry uncontrollably. What was wrong with Quan? Why was he in America, and did the company send him there? But why? He didn't know his parents were both dead. Her mind went blank. It was just too much information to take in all at once, as she was overloaded with grief. She fell to the floor, where she lay until it grew dark. Then she dragged herself to her bed and cried herself to sleep. She woke later in the morning, and it all came flooding back. She had to get to Chen and tell him about Quan's letter. What was Quan doing in America? Chen was her comforter.

After having given Chen Quan's letter, he was just as mystified as Jia Li as to why the company had sent him to America and his friend to France. Why was he not allowed to contact his parents? That seemed really strange, and what were the tourist places he was meant to visit? But was he still alive, or had he succumbed to the illness? None of this made sense. "Did Quan ever talk to your parents about going to America? Did he have money of his own to pay his way?" he asked Jia Li. "No, this is a shock as he never wanted to travel because he was frightened of flying. He certainly didn't have any money of his own. Why was he not allowed to contact my parents? They were heartbroken when he didn't come home." They looked at each other with blank expressions on their faces. It was time for Chen to tell what he had learnt at the market from one of the guards. "But why would so many people from your company die?" she asked. Chen was puzzled by Jia Li's question, but she had a point! "Do you think Quan is going to be okay? I'm frightened that his pneumonia will be the virus, and how will we know what has happened to him?" sobbed Jia Li. Chen didn't want to make known what he was thinking, "We will have to wait and see if he makes contact again."

4

RESTRICTIONS FOR ALL

THEN THE NEWS that shocked the world. There were border restrictions imposed, countries banned international flights, and no-one wanted people from China entering their country because that was where the virus was thought to have originated. It was as if the world had shut down completely, apart from the virus, which was rampant, choking the universe from all directions. The big questions were how did it spread to so many countries so quickly and what was the cause? How did the virus originate? This was the question on everyone's mind. Different stories circulated. In the papers each day a new theory came to light, but these were purely guesses; no-one had a clue!

The only two people who knew more than anyone outside the actual conspiracy was Chen and Jia Li. Perhaps the letter from Quan held vital clues, as this information was not meant to be revealed. It was all meant to be classified as confidential to the company, but a leak had occurred. Chen thought hard on this and confided in Jia Li, reminding her their lives could be in danger if this information left their hands. Again, they were drawn together in a frightening situation.

Chen helped Jia Li to finish sorting out her belongings at her flat as he didn't want her to be alone. He was afraid for them both, so best they stayed together so he could protect her. She made arrangements with a neighbour to collect any mail that was put in her letterbox and she would call and check often, hoping she would hear from Quan again. Although she clung to hope, a feeling deep down in her heart told her otherwise, but at this moment, hope was all she could focus on. Her life was nothing but a nightmare, and if not for Chen what would she have done?

With the market closed and border restrictions in place, they could not venture outside their house. China closed everything down, and outside drones hovered above the streets yelling at people to get inside. Elsewhere facial recognition software, linked to a mandatory phone app based on contagion risk, decided who could enter shopping malls and public spaces. Masks were mandatory. Chen had a little money from his parents so they stocked up on food items because they were forced into a 'lockdown', as neither wanted to catch the virus which had now been classified as a world pandemic. Each day the restrictions became harder to accept; now people were confined to their homes and if outside the home for specific reasons, they had to observe social distancing.

The world was in a mess and still no positive feedback on how it was all started, other than it began in China, as did the SARS virus. China's authorities had kept it a secret, thus causing ill-feeling in the rest of the world. The World Health Organisation themselves didn't recognise this to be a pandemic until it was apparent, and by then the warnings came too late. Initially WHO advocated against limiting travel with China and recommended that countries keep borders open. This organisation lavished praise on China, which was unnecessary and wrong. Did WHO need China on its side, as it rose to become the next superpower? Did the virus now have the world in its grasp?

Chen listened to the news, as with each day came new claims as to what had caused the pandemic. The first thought was that it was linked to bats, as this virus was the same strain found in these animals. But it was mentioned that as there were very few bats at the market in the past few days, perhaps the virus had mutated and jumped to a second party who was the actual infected carrier. No-one knew the animal in which the virus had mutated, but if this particular animal had been consumed as food, this was where the virus began. This was the only explanation at this time. This was qualified by an article in the newspaper that said: 'Most viruses are specialists; they establish long associations with preferred host species. Occasionally viruses will emerge or spill over from the original hosts to a new host. When this happens the risk of disease increases. Most infectious diseases are the result of a spill-over from wild organisms – bats, pangolins – which are considered a delicacy in China and in other Asian countries.' This was all news to Chen, as with everyday life in poor areas, the cheaper the food the more is consumed. Price dictates what food people can afford to buy, so choice all comes down to money.

At this stage this thought was on everyone's mind. No-one knew otherwise, so everyone went along with the status quo. It did not help or stop the coronavirus now known as Covid-19, as its spread was now catastrophic in America, France, Italy and many other countries. People were developing pneumonia-type symptoms, mostly the elderly, who were dying in their hundreds. It did not seem to be affecting the younger generation, although it was first thought they may be carriers. Chen squirmed at the thought of bats being the main source, as he knew there were bats at his workplace. He asked himself whether this was where the virus began but then escaped. No-one outside his workplace knew what experiments were being carried on behind closed doors in the laboratories, even the workers at the company didn't know. Were the officials looking at the wrong source for where it started? He talked with Jia Li and told her all he knew; he had to tell someone as it was burning in his brain. They had the same thought: was his workplace the offender? This prompted Chen to make notes to record his findings, as they may be handy in the future. "Do you think we were carriers of the virus to our parents?" asked Jia Li. Chen thought for a moment, "Not you, Jia Li, but your brother and I both worked for the company, so we may have been guilty of this. I can't understand why I haven't become sick; this is a mystery."

Several days later a new theory appeared in the newspaper. It was thought the virus may have been contracted through wildlife mixing with domestic animals. Many other coronaviruses exist naturally in wild mammals and bird populations around the world. Human interaction drives the emergence of new disease-causing viruses as humans push back the boundaries of the last wild places on earth. Species that evolved separately were now mixing. Also, global markets allow free trade of live animals including their eggs, semen and meat. Given the enormous number of viruses that exist, our willingness to provide them with global transport spelt disaster! Future spill-overs are inevitable, this should tell us ... leave wildlife in the wild! This was another theory that could have begun in Chen's workplace, as he remembered when the boy's dog attacked the bat, this was a case of domestic versus wild animals. This second scenario also tied in with his workplace, unknown to the outside world. Chen's notes were growing, and so was his fear of what lay ahead.

● 5

FEELINGS RELEASED

Meanwhile there was a relationship forming between Chen and Jia Li. With each day she came further out of her shell and smiled more often, which made him feel happy. She leaned on him for support when the chips were down and a growing self-respect allowed her to open up and share her thoughts. They even held hands as they sat opposite each other at the table. Sometimes she took the initiative and made the first move which delighted Chen, as then he could see it wasn't all one-sided. The warmth inside him was heating up and he hoped she felt the same feelings. Only time would tell; at this stage he felt things could not be rushed!

Today Chen and Jia Li decided to walk down to his old workplace to see what was happening. He hoped to see someone he knew. As they were nearing the site, Chen spotted his workmate Tan, the man who he had gone into the wilds with. "Hi, Tan," he called. With this Tan came over to talk to him. "Did you know the company was going to close down before it did?" asked Chen. "No, but something was wrong there. So many of my workmates have died or gone missing, and no-one knows what has happened to them. Do you know? I only know of two of the laboratory workers who have survived, one of them being my brother. I don't know if any scientists are still alive. No-one ever asked what was going on in the laboratory for fear of losing their jobs, but now I wonder." Chen panicked: should he tell Tan what he knew? Could he trust him? "I had no idea; I didn't know so many workers died. I think something strange was happening there, I have my theory, but until I find out more, I will keep it to myself. One thing I do know is that all the Saturday workers were given an injection, but no other workers were. Why?" "Funny you should mention that, as they are the workers that are missing," answered Tan. Chen's head started swirling and fear was mounting. Then Tan told him that his brother was one of the heads of the pharmaceutical department and when he questioned him, he was told not to take it any further. "I mentioned about you working with me and he told me not to meet with you again." Chen decided not to mention Quan after hearing this. It would stay as his and Jia Li's secret. "Could we meet in a fortnight's time to see if we have any more information for each other?" he asked. Both parties agreed to this.

That night all was quiet in Chen's house. Jia Li was lying on her bed rethinking the day's events, especially the conversation between Chen and Tan. She thought it was strange that only the Saturday boys were given the flu vaccine, then pieces from Quan's letter came back to haunt her. What places was he meant to visit and why? Was he ever going to come back? She called out to Chen to come and sit on the bed with her, as she wanted to tell him what was circulating in her mind. He knocked on her door and waited to be asked in. "You don't have to knock; this is your house, Chen." "But this is your bedroom, and I respect that you must have privacy. I would feel bad entering without your permission." "You are such a decent man. Come and lie with me," she asked. As they lay together, she told him her thoughts. Then she moved closer to him and placed his arm on her breast. Immediately warmth welled up inside him and he knew at that moment he had fallen in love with her. Did she feel the same? He cradled her in his arms, and she responded by pulling him closer to her; this let him know the answer. His hands slid inside her blouse and he felt her soft skin and the shape of her breasts. She responded by squeezing his buttocks, and there her hands lingered until he took them and put them on his genital area. Jia Li had never been this far with a man so was at a loss as to what to do next. "Have you made love before?" he asked her. "This is my first time and I want it to happen." He asked her to undress as he would do, then to climb into bed. Neither looked at each other's body, as shyness was an issue for them both. They cuddled into each other, both feeling strange body parts against their skin. The excitement mounted for Chen and he took the lead, gently touching her and preparing her for what was about to happen. Jia

Li had read what happened between a man and woman, but to experience it was a pleasure no-one could describe. She knew at that moment she loved Chen and fell asleep in his arms.

Chen stirred first the next morning and was happy to find Jia Li still asleep in his arms. He had waited for so long to take her but would only do so with her approval; it had to be a two-way affair. He had thought he would never find love again, but it had happened, and for this he was truly grateful. He felt there was no disrespect to his last love, but to have the chance to love again was a blessing. He lay still until Jia Li stirred as he didn't want to disturb her, in case she regretted what they had done. She looked at Chen and smiled, which was what he hoped would happen! Now there were no secrets between them; they were united in every way.

The paperwork was mounting but there were still so many questions to be answered. They worked out the missing boys must have been sent to different countries, but the reason eluded them. Why were they vaccinated when no-one else was? This was what they could not work out. The world news was bringing very little joy, as now a second wave of the virus had emerged and it was worse than the first, as thousands of people were dying, with no end in sight. Where was the world heading, Chen asked himself? This was history happening before their very eyes in this year 2020, when the world changed forever. Would the word 'normal' ever surface again?

A fortnight had passed and Chen was looking forward to his next meeting with Tan as was arranged. Both he and

Jia Li waited anxiously at the old workplace, but as the time slipped by, he started to worry. Suddenly a lady appeared and asked, "Are you Chen? I am Tan's wife. He gave me a letter to pass onto you before he died." Chen stood dumfounded. Tan dead? What had happened to him? "Did he die of the virus?" he asked. "No, he didn't catch the virus, but he must have eaten something that poisoned his system. He had a quick death and was in terrible pain, but he found time to write you this letter, which he asked me to give you, so here I am." Chen thanked her for coming and offered his and Jai Li's condolences. "Can you manage without your husband?" he asked. "It will be hard as we have three children, but so many people like us are suffering, and it is something we have to live with and try to move on." With these words she left. Chen grasped the letter tight in his hands; what was he going to learn? He would not open it until he got home when he and Jia Li would read it together.

The letter began: 'Chen, I spoke with a survivor who worked in the laboratory and he told me they were designing a virus to spread around the world as a deterrent to other countries: don't interfere in China's politics or else! The missing boys were sent to different countries to spread the virus. I have no evidence, but this is what I have worked out. That is why they were given injections; it was not a flu injection but a virus one. My brother called to visit. He was selling a health product that he wanted me to try. It was then I fell sick. Take care my friend and goodbye. Tan' As Chen read this, tears flowed down his cheeks and Jia Li could see he was grief-stricken.

She waited for him to recover then asked, "Is this why the boys were sent to different countries. It makes me sick to think they may have been injected with the virus; this would mean they were never going to come home. Oh, Chen, how sad. Quan would have died of the deadly virus not long after writing his letter." She sat in shock trying to digest it all. How appalling of the company!

After Chen took it all in, he suddenly jumped up and went to his bedroom and brought out his file with all the cuttings he had collected. He remembered reading that most of the passengers on a flight from China to America arrived unwell. Was this the same time Quan said he fell sick on his flight? If so, was this the start of the virus reaching America? Then a more sinister thought took over: were the boys in fact injected with the virus then sent home to their families so they would catch the virus and die, and so no-one would be left to question their disappearance? Surely the company wouldn't be so ruthless towards its own countrymen, but if orders came from a higher source, in politics nothing stood in the way.

That night Chen and Jia Li went to bed and lay in each other's arms. This was the only place on earth they felt safe. Their bedroom was their haven, their sanctuary, where they could find happiness, as outside of this room, so much heartache loomed. Jia Li was thankful she had found a lover in Chen. He taught her how to share her feelings, and they made love countless times, as this took them to a happy place where there were no boundaries or interference! Their lives had become entwined with secrets only they knew and could not share with anyone else. Would the time ever arrive when they could tell the world the truth … where this all began?

Chen read the papers each day and was horrified at how the pandemic was played down in his country. Was China using this crisis as an opportunity to shut off the outside world? The response to Covid-19 was being reported from the authorities in Beijing. He knew that thousands of his people were filling the hospitals, which were better equipped than most worldwide, because of the SARS outbreak a few years earlier. This had them prepared for future viral outbreaks so ventilators, masks and PPE equipment were readily available, which saved many lives. Not so in other countries, as Chen was horrified to read about the shortages of emergency equipment in highly developed countries such as America, Europe and Britain, thus causing thousands of unnecessary deaths. He wondered if his country was able to help out in a crisis. But sadly, this had become political. Was China exploiting the virus for its political propaganda war against the United States? Mr Trump had threatened to remove Chinese firms from Wall Street, and this spelt trouble. Also, Trump was accusing China in front of the whole world of starting the virus and he would not let go of this; it made him feel important. Thus, the US–China fight wasn't going away anytime soon!

6

A BOMBSHELL

TODAY CHEN RECEIVED a letter from an undisclosed source, which was circulating around the city but hidden from the authorities. If the source was found, heads would roll – literally! A Nobel Prize-winning professor of medicine from a foreign country stated that China was lying and one day the truth would be revealed. He stated: 'The coronavirus is not natural; it is a manufactured virus and completely artificial, as it would not have adversely affected the entire world in this way. It would have spread in hot places and died in cold places or vice versa. I worked with the laboratory staff at this pharmaceutical company several years ago and have tried for three months to contact them, but their phones are all dead. It is understood they have all died.' Chen froze on reading this article. Here were his findings brought out in the open, and he was relieved he wasn't the only one who knew the truth. But would this ever be revealed? Who was this brave soul? Chen feared for him, but commended him at the same time. Was there going to be a connection? He prayed their paths would cross one day.

Eventually the authorities got 'whiff' of this paper and they were outraged. There was no proof and they certainly didn't want their people to believe in this propaganda. Chen searched all the papers and cut out articles relevant to the 'why and when' of the virus outbreak. It had consumed his and Jia Li's lives for the past few months, but now it was falling into place. Their secret was shared by someone else and now it was out there, be it underground. They had even thought of leaving China, but the borders were still closed, so they couldn't escape to a safer sanctuary.

As the restrictions were slowly lifting, Chen and Jia Li saw people on the streets asking for help. These were migrant workers who had become outcasts without any access to state benefits or protection. The authorities did not make a direct cash infusion to any workers. Most of these migrant workers lived in rural areas but had come to the city for factory work. They were caught up in lockdown, were not able to return to their homes and were in no position to keep themselves, with no work and their savings dwindling. All factories were closed down, so no workers were required. These migrant workers were left destitute, forced to beg on the streets.

Chen was interested in the reports in the papers, because he learnt all sectors of the economy were indeed suffering. Many of the tech-related businesses were hit hard by the economic crash caused by the pandemic, so it wasn't only the factory workers it affected but skilled workers and big companies too. Was his company one of them? A little light shone on the digital economy, gaming, on-line education and meal deliveries.

But Chen knew China was an important manufacturing centre for the world and would continue its growth momentum faster than any other country. He and Jia Li along with millions of other people would just have to manage until jobs became available. He was thrilled to read that China had agreed to supply desperately needed medical equipment to the rest of the world. Also, a tech billionaire, the co-founder of Alibaba, Jack Ma, donated millions of dollars' worth of medical equipment to Africa.

Some days Chen would notice Jia Li sitting with tears in her eyes staring up at the sky and he knew she was thinking of her brother, Quan. She often had nightmares of his last days alone in a strange city somewhere in America suffering with the virus and no-one by his side. But worst of all, to have spread the virus that caused so many deaths would have been the last straw, as he was a gentle soul. Jia Li could not get this thought out of her head; it haunted her. Why did his company even think of such a horrid act, introducing a virus to the world through innocent young lads, all because their country didn't want any outside interference? Why, she asked herself, did so many innocent people have to pay this price? Where was the justice in this?

The unrest between China and its neighbouring territory was drawing interest from the rest of the world, thus the warning: 'Don't interfere or there will be consequences'. People living in the neighbouring territory were living a free life, allowed to voice their opinions. This China didn't like, as it was outside communist reform. Jia Li found this vendetta against innocent people inexcusable, especially against the elderly who weren't interested in politics, and they were the age group the virus was affecting most. The world was still on edge as America and the United Kingdom were experiencing record daily deaths. When was the virus going to go away?

Many times, Chen and Jia Li went back to Chen's old workplace, although it had been cordoned off with high fences, hoping to see a worker lingering there, but no, this was not to be, and luck was not on their side. Had they all died as was mentioned in the secret report? If so, he counted himself lucky to still be alive. There were many deserted houses around that area. Had they moved away or had they in fact died of the virus? The known truth, as such, was that the market was where the virus started, and any other suggestions were quashed before they made the media. But Chen knew the media was controlled by the powers that be, because in China everything was controlled. That was why they could not make their findings public. Their lives would be in danger, they would just disappear like all the rest who had a voice. As did the head of emergency at the Xihun Central Hospital, who first alerted authorities about the virus. She had not been seen since, and probably had been detained by the Chinese government … or worse! Some days it was hard for them to read the untruths being fed to the people. The government knew the truth and that is where it was going to stay. The American president Mr Trump was the only person to stand up to China. He blamed them for all sorts of lies. He even suggested it was a manufactured virus, but because of his stupidity with words, no-one took any notice! No-one except Chen and Jia Li! Mr Trump was upset as he recognised the long-term economic impact on businesses and schools in America. He immediately announced a suspension of Washington's financial contribution to the WHO, which stunned the world, as America was its largest financier. Was this virus designed so as to weaken the United States, and the liberal order, so that China's ascent would be accelerated.

7

A NEW LEAD

ONE DAY while out shopping Chen saw in the distance a face he thought was familiar. He made his way over to the young lady and as he got nearer, he recognised her as one of the front office girls from the company. As she was about to leave the shopping centre, he noticed something strange in the way she walked; it was almost as if she had had a stroke. She seemed to be dragging her right leg. He was shocked as he remembered her as a sprightly young lady who greeted all the workers at the beginning of their working day. Chen didn't know if he should speak to her, but this was the first workmate he had seen since being made redundant, other than Tan, who was no longer alive! "Excuse me Miss, did you use to work for the pharmaceutical company next door to the market?" She slowly turned to face him, "I know you," she cried. Before Chen could say anything, she kept on talking, "Are you alright, did anything happen to you? Look at me, I caught the virus and after two weeks in hospital this is what I am left with," as she pointed to her leg. "All my workmates have died; I have even lost my parents. You are the only one from our work that I know has survived. I think it is because we worked so close to the market that we all caught the virus." Poor Chen, what could he say! "Surely you must have known someone that survived as you knew everyone at work?" he asked. "I have tried ringing people, but their phones are all dead. I don't know where they lived so I couldn't visit them to see if they were still alive."

Chen told her about Tan. Then he mentioned that for many days following the closedown he and his partner had gone back to the company's yard hoping to see someone, but to no avail. He continued, "Do you know if many of the stallholders from the market survived?" "Yes, I have brought things from several of them. They set up in different places to try to get sales. Isn't it strange how some of them have survived, when most of our company's workers have died; you would think they would be affected worse than us?" Was this the final nail in the coffin for Chen? This is what the Nobel Prize winner mentioned about the company's workers, dead phone lines, and no contact able to be made. Were they in fact all dead?

Now it was up to Chen to track down the remaining stallholders at their new marketplaces and start asking questions. "Did you know before the company closed down that all the staff were given an injection to protect them against the flu? Even I was one of them," she told Chen. "How strange they didn't ask me?" he said. "Probably because you worked in the nursery, and you were nothing to do with the pharmaceutical side," came the answer. Chen was left perplexed, then a sudden horrifying thought came to his mind. Did the company in fact inject everyone with the virus so that they would die and no secrets could be revealed, but they would stay within the higher powers. A chill passed down his spine! Here was this poor girl partially paralysed; had the injection caused this? He had to ask, "What actually happened to you?" "Two days after my injection, my parents and I fell ill. I tried to look after them, but they passed away together, then my respiratory system shut down. I don't remember what happened for over a week, and when I came around in hospital, this is what had happened to me. I'm so sad," she sobbed. Chen reached out and took her hand until the sobbing stopped. "I'm sorry, I am grateful I have survived in spite of my disability." Chen asked if they could meet again, as he didn't want to break this friendship, with her being his only contact from his workplace. Perhaps she might remember more as the days went past. It was agreed that they would meet again at the same place in two weeks' time. Before they parted Chen asked where the old stallholders had set up, as he wanted to visit them.

He couldn't wait to get home and tell Jia Li about meeting the young lady from his workplace. As he burst through the door, no Jia Li was there to greet him. He ran to the bedroom only to find her sprawled across the bed in terrible pain. "What is wrong?" he asked, as he bent down to calm her. Through her sobs she managed to get out that something was happening inside her body; it was burning. Chen called the hospital, but they were full and were taking no more patients, but they agreed to send a doctor. He sat with Jia Li as she wreathed in pain. Tears were sliding down his cheeks; he could do nothing to help her. Chen tucked her into bed and lay beside her holding her hand, hoping the doctor would arrive soon.

The doctor duly arrived and examined Jia Li but the symptoms were not that of the virus but something that was attacking her body at an alarming rate. He took a blood sample and gave her an injection to help ease the pain. He told Chen he would ring him as soon as he knew what was causing her illness. It didn't take him long to ring back and tell him it was poisoning. She had eaten something that had poisoned her system, and there was nothing they could do. He would come back on his way home from the hospital and check on her. Chen thought back to what she had eaten that he hadn't, and he remembered the health food the man had sold her. She ate it for breakfast, but he refused it; was this the silent killer? He watched as she struggled to breathe then her breaths became fewer and fewer. Here lay his soulmate, the only person who he shared his secrets with. He prayed that God would spare her, but sadly his prayers were not answered. By the time the doctor arrived Jia Li had passed away and he found Chen lying sobbing on their bed. "Do you know what could have caused this, what she might have eaten?" he asked. Chen didn't want to talk. His loved one had gone, and what would he tell the doctor?

Next morning, the van pulled up at the door to take Jia Li's body away, to be buried in a mass grave alongside other virus victims. The fear of disease was rampant so all bodies had to be buried as soon as possible. Chen went straight to the shops and bought face masks, as he had to keep protecting himself against the virus. He spent many hours lying on his bed wishing Jia Li was there with him; he missed her terribly. Once again, he was alone in his house. As the days passed, he felt miserable and lost. He had almost given up the will to live. Then his mind began focusing on the man who had sold the health food. Who was he? Did he know something? Was it Chen himself who was meant to be poisoned or perhaps both of them? Then they would be silenced forever. These thoughts kept swirling around in his head. Where to from here? he asked himself.

The day was getting nearer to when he had arranged to meet the young lady from his workplace. This brought a little glimmer of hope to his heart, for at least he knew someone, and he wasn't as alone as he thought. But before his meeting with her, he decided to go the new markets and talk to the stallholders who had survived the virus. They had set up on the other side of the city in a small way and no livestock was present. The thought of the virus having started from animals made people very wary, but Chen knew different! He immediately recognised several of the people from the previous market. One man in particular he knew quite well so approached him, hoping for information. "Hi, I remember you. You're from the old market. Why have you set up here?" "I need to feed my surviving children. My wife and mother died from the virus." Chen offered his condolences then asked. "Do you know of many stallholders who have survived?" "There are still a few of us, perhaps less than half, but I heard the pharmaceutical workers are all gone apart from a crippled young lady and now yourself. Some used to live in this area, but none have come to buy from us; perhaps they are all gone." "Does that not strike you as strange?" asked Chen. The man looked at him vaguely and scratched his head, "We just thought they blamed us for the virus and decided not to buy from us." Chen had to fight hard to hold back from spilling the truth. The wrong people were getting the blame, but that suited the authorities right down to the ground. With this he brought some vegetables then headed home. While home on his own, he often wondered why Jia Li died of food poisoning. Who was the man who sold her the health food at their front door? He had not come since, which he thought was strange. Was this a random one-off sale where they both were meant to die? This made him cringe. Who was out there, and did they know what he knew? But he had been careful who he talked to.

Today was the day Chen was meeting the young lady from his old workplace, at the shopping centre, as was arranged. He had mixed feelings as to what he was going to discuss with her. Did she have a right to know what had gone on in their company? He would suss her out before making any decisions, as he knew he had to be careful who he shared his information with. This was when he missed Jia Li most; he had no-one to share his thoughts or talk with. She had been his soulmate, and he loved her, but sadly she was no-more! As he was waiting for the young woman, he tried to remember her name, but it eluded him. All he knew was she was a bright friendly soul who knew most of the workers in the pharmaceutical department and he was deeply upset to see her as a cripple. These weren't the memories he had of her in the past. Where did she live? he wondered.

Then he saw her dragging her leg as she made her way towards him, "Hi Chen, I'm so happy you decided to come," she called to him. He greeted her and was surprised that her happy personality was still there. "I'm sorry but I can't think of your name?" he told her. "I'm Lan Mei. Fancy forgetting that," she teased him. They walked to a nearby café and sat down. Chen asked her if she would like a drink so they both ordered tea. He told her he had spoken with some of the market people and almost half of them were still alive. "But they knew most of our workers had died. Doesn't that seem strange when the virus started in the marketplace?" Lan Mei hesitated. "I've been thinking about this for some time and am mystified as to why so many of our people are either dead or missing. You did know some of our Saturday boys went missing? I had to sign them off the payroll. In fact many were given a good bonus then they disappeared. I can't for the life of me understand where they went. Do you know where they are?" she asked Chen.

Chen knew from this conversation he could talk to her. "My girlfriend's brother was one of the Saturday lads who went missing. She received a letter from him and he was in America." Then he proceeded to tell her the whole story. Lan Mei listened and her eyes widened as he spoke his thoughts. "Really Chen, do you think the company was that bad? Oh my God, what are we going to do? Perhaps the bonus the boys received must have been the payment needed for them to go overseas. How did your girlfriend cope with learning that about her brother?" She watched as tears appeared in his eyes. "Jai-li died nearly two weeks ago of food poisoning. I miss her so much," he sobbed. Lan Mei leaned over and touched his arm. "I'm so sorry, but you can't give up. Look at me, I'm a cripple but I have survived, and life must go on." Chen was taken by her tenacity. She was such a brave person considering her disability, but he knew she was right: he couldn't give up now!

"Where are you living?" Chen asked Lan Mei. She told him she was living in a boarding house and sharing a room with whoever arrived at night, sometimes two, sometimes three girls, but it was all she could afford. She was just happy to have a place to put her head down. He felt really sad for her; she expected very little from life. "Would you like to come and live at my house? You would have your own bedroom." he said. "Can I come and have a look?" After they finished their tea, they walked slowly to his house, and he couldn't help but notice her dragging her leg, but this didn't seem to dampen her spirit. Once they arrived, Chen showed her through and she was happy with what she saw – her own bedroom, how wonderful! She didn't know Chen all that well, but she could sense he was a decent man. "How much do you want for the room?" she asked. "There is no charge for the room, if you have spare money perhaps you can help share the food costs?" Lan Mei was ecstatic. She told him she loved cooking so would make up for the rent by cooking his meals. "When can I come?" They agreed that Chen would come to her place next Saturday and he would load her gear on to his bike. She was so excited.

A week later and Lan Mei was living in Chen's house. She was loving every minute, so did Chen, as she cooked his meals and fussed over him. Her disability was forgotten, and nothing was a bother for her. She was just a normal girl who didn't let anything interfere with her life. Chen was amazed how she coped with life in general, and he didn't see her as a handicapped person; he saw her for what she was, a happy and capable young lady who made him laugh.

The time had come for Chen to talk over his 'conspiracy' thoughts. Lan Mei had contributed snippets as she remembered unusual incidents that had happened at work. They were helping Chen put pieces together and the prognosis did not look good for the company. It was still believed that the virus was started at the market, and any other suggestions were quashed by the authorities. A second wave of the virus had struck many cities, crippling their economy. People's lives had changed, and so many elderly had died because of the lack of ventilators; those that had access to them survived, but for the rest it was a lottery! China was over the worst as they were prepared and had the needed equipment. Chen didn't think the numbers who died were correctly reported to the media, but this was controlled by government authorities in Beijing. This was how China worked: truths and propaganda were as one. The authorities were tight-lipped to the rest of the world. Chen had time to learn many things that he was oblivious to before, but now he read the newspapers and they were his main source of information, although most of it was based around China. America was on the outer, and Mr Trump's Twitter stupidity, right or wrong, was brushed off as a joke.

One day Lan Mei noticed a man loitering outside their house. It wasn't the first time she had seen him, but it was only now it registered that she had seen him there before. She called Chen to come and have a look to see if he knew him. He looked out the window at the man, and yes, he remembered him as the salesman who had sold Jia Li the health food. 'What is he doing back here?' Chen wondered. Something about the man made him think he had seen his face prior to him coming to their door as a salesman, but where? More to the point, why was he back? Did he know something? He told Lan Mei that if he came to the door when he wasn't home, to purchase what he was selling but not to eat it. He would take it and get it analysed, to see if it contained a poisonous substance. This would give him a clue as to what his intentions were. He walked over to his chair and sat down then closed his eyes, trying to visualise that face, wondering where he had seen it before, but his mind went blank, and nothing was forthcoming.

The following day as Chen took out his bike to go to the shops, he noticed the same man standing a little further down the street. Is he watching to see if I leave the house, he wondered? He cycled around the corner and waited for a few moments then backtracked, only to see the man at his front door. He saw Lan Mei take something from him and within minutes he was gone. He continued to the shops but didn't linger, as he wanted to see what he had sold her. On arriving back, he was met at the door. "Chen, that man called and asked me to buy his latest health food. It's on the bench wrapped in plastic." Chen picked it up carefully, so as not to make contact with the ingredients in the wrapping. "Tomorrow I will take it and have it analysed just to satisfy my own curiosity as I'm sure that is what poisoned Jia Li. I'll have to be discreet; I'll say it was given to me for my dog and I want it checked out first." "But we don't have a dog, Chen." remarked Lan Mei. This brought a smile to Chen's face.

At the enquiry counter, in the veterinary section of the animal health centre, Chen asked to speak with somebody that handled the testing of animal food. A young man appeared so Chen spoke with him. "I was given some food for my dog by a neighbour, but as he has complained about him in the past, I am afraid he might want to poison him. Could you check to see if this is safe?" "Certainly, just take a seat while I do a test," he told Chen and Lan Mei. Chen's brain was still trying to fathom out who the man was, where he had seen him before, but still it eluded him. He was suddenly awakened from his thoughts by the young man. "Just as well you brought this in to be tested sir, it would have killed your dog, as it is laced with arsenic. We will keep it here and destroy it. Will you tell us who the man was that gave it to you?" Chen declined, saying he didn't want to cause any trouble in his neighbourhood. With this they thanked him and left. Chen felt sick; this was obviously the cause of Jia Li's death. It frightened him, and his worst fears were realised. Someone was out to get rid of him. But what about Lan Mei? She was innocent; was it safe for her to stay in his house? He would have to discuss this with her.

Chen and Lan Mei sat down to talk over what was happening, as he was worried for her safety. "Perhaps it would be better for you to live somewhere else where it was safe," he told her. "I will never leave you, Chen. You have been so kind to me, and we are in this together. You may not have noticed, as it is not long since you lost Jia Li, but you make me feel whole, you have looked past my disability and seen me as a woman, for this I want you to know I have deep feelings for you and hope you will feel the same about me one day. I will wait for however long it takes." Chen was stunned! He hadn't thought romantically since Jia Li's death. Had he not let go, or did he blame himself for her death? The answer was yes to both questions. Lan Mei saw the pain in his eyes and realised he was still not over Jia Li. "I will be there when the time is right," and she reached for his hand. They looked at each other and Chen smiled in acknowledgement of what had just been put before him.

Now he knew someone was out to silence him: it was the salesman. That feeling came back to haunt him – where had he seen him before? He went to bed with the face imprinted in his mind and lay for hours trying to recollect where he might have seen him. Then suddenly the penny dropped. It wasn't his image he was seeing it was that of his workmate Tan. He was Tan's lookalike, and he remembered something Tan had told him. He had a brother who was head of the pharmaceutical department in the laboratory and who had warned Tan not to discuss work-related things with Chen. But why was this man trailing him? He didn't even know him. Did Tan say something that may have incriminated him? Perhaps Lan Mei would know more about him as she was the office girl for that department. He would have to wait until morning to find out.

At the breakfast table Chen told Lan Mei about Tan's brother. Could she remember him? She certainly knew him as he was an outspoken man who liked to be in control. "But why didn't I recognise him?" she asked herself. Then she thought back to what he was wearing: a long coat and a hat pulled down over his eyes. This would be so he wasn't recognisable. "I wonder if he remembered me?" asked Lan Mei. If he had, then the two of them would be in danger! It was now obvious most of the pharmaceutical staff had died, or rather been given an injection so they would succumb to the virus, and then no questions could be asked. But no-one foresaw that one of the lads had written home and told of his whereabouts, plus a few extra details, enough to follow up on.

After having this discussion, Chen and Lan Mei decided they would only eat food they bought themselves at the supermarket, and they would be very vigilant while consuming foodstuffs. If this was the company's plan of attack, they would not end up as victims. Hopefully this would be where it ended!

8

THE COMPANY, NOW THE 'ESTABLISHMENT'

MEANWHILE, since the laboratory closed down, several of the chemists and pharmaceutical assistants, along with government officials who were protected from the virus, had set up secret headquarters where they monitored the progress of the virus outcome. All the young men they sent abroad had stuck to their itinerary, and this was proven with the spread of the virus. They knew none of them had survived as no-one claimed a return ticket after the month was up, but of course this was the plan, to have no survivors. Little did they know one lad had broken the rules and had contacted his family with enough information to spark an investigation. The injection was a strain of the virus given to the boys who were then sent home to their family for a night, just enough time for their household to contract it. This was a calculated measure to take out the families so no questions could be asked when the boys didn't return. By the time the month was up, all elderly parents would have died.

They watched as the virus took over the world and was wiping out mostly elderly people, but that didn't matter; they were no use to anyone, they were costing too much money to keep alive. Also, the lower-class dwellers and the weak had become a burden on society, so if it affected others, then that was plain bad luck! The weak would die and the healthy would survive to breed a healthy race of people – no use breeding from the weak! This was China's opportunity to shut off the outside world and exploit Western weaknesses, especially America, who were against the uprising in China's neighbouring territory. Of course, this was meant to be an in-house take-over, without outside interference, but human rights groups led the protest, causing all sorts of problems for China. Neighbouring Taiwan was also a target for China as they were trying to take it over and bring it under communist rule.

But in spite of their expectations, the virus was spiralling out of control, and it was now a world pandemic! China could see it had mutated beyond their reckoning and was causing unforeseen problems. Something as huge as this had never been seen since the bubonic plague. Had man outwitted himself?

This was the time for China to start its economy growing again, by producing medical equipment for the rest of the world. It had in reserve its own respiratory supplies, an overflow from the SARS virus, so it was partially prepared, perhaps the only country that was.

Now began the task of producing all medical supplies needed – masks, ventilators and PPE clothing – for the rest of the world, who were relying on China for this help. Was this the plan to make the rest of the world dependent on China? Is this the recognition they wanted? But one thing was for sure, their friendship with America had soured, as the virus was seen as a political propaganda war against this country. Mr Trump was making wild accusations against China, none of which was believed, but had he in fact hit on the truth?

The days that followed felt long and arduous for Chen and Lan Mei, but where to from here? They were two insignificant persons who knew more than they were meant to, and now their lives were in danger. Had Tan talked to his brother about Chen's findings? What did he actually know? All they could do was be patient and see if the man came back. Chen thought hard on this and decided to put a plan in place to make it happen. He told Lan Mei, "We are probably being watched. I will stay inside and not be seen by the outside world. It will be as if I have died. Are you happy to do this?" She agreed as life was becoming a little frightening for them both.

It only took several days to pass before Lan Mei noticed the same man loitering outside their house. This went on for another week, and each day he walked past, stopped, looked in, then carried on. In the meantime, Chen had plenty of time to think, as he didn't much care for being house-bound. His mind focused on Lan Mei and what a happy soul she was. She brought joy and laughter into his life, but above all, she was extremely brave. Her disability was forgotten, there wasn't anything she couldn't do and he realised she had become a big part of his life. Was he ready to let his head rule his heart? Had the time come for him to ask her to share his bed? He could think of nothing better than to wake up each morning with her in his arms. These thoughts were happening more often, so perhaps the time had come. Suddenly his concentration was broken by Lan Mei. "Chen, the man is coming to the door. What will I do?" Chen thought for a moment and told her to invite him in, then he would deal to him. Instantly he knew what had to happen, but he wouldn't tell Lan Mei. He went into the bedroom and grabbed a hammer that was hidden under his bed.

Lan Mei went to the door to answer the knock. There before her stood the same man, and now she knew who he was. Yes, that was definitely the man from her workplace. She invited him in. He stood and looked around before asking her if she was alone. "Yes, Chen has passed away." "How much do you know?" he questioned her. "I know about the conspiracy and where the virus started, that the company was involved. Chen had put it all together." With this he grabbed her from behind and pulled her arms behind her back. "I'll get rid of you also, then no-one will know other than the people involved." From out of the bedroom, Chen charged with the hammer in his hand. "Let go of her you animal, you will be the one got rid of," and he hit him over the head with the hammer. He fell in a heap on the floor. "You've killed him, Chen," she screamed. He took her in his arms. "It's alright Lan

Mei, if he is dead then that's what he deserves. Our life will be different with him gone. Don't feel sorry for him; look at all the lives they have taken, hundreds and thousands of innocent people. His life is worthless." Lan Mei listened to what Chen had said. Yes, he was right, this man deserved to die, so many others didn't!

Chen picked up the basket from the floor as the ingredients had fallen out, so he carefully put them back in and placed the basket on the bench. While doing this he heard a groan and looked around – the man was not dead. He fetched a rope and tied his hands behind his back. There was blood flowing from his head where the hammer came in contact with his skull. Chen couldn't stand to look at him so dragged him to the washroom and left him on the concrete floor. He could suffer alone, so he shut the door. Lan Mei cleaned the blood off the wooden floor, but she was still a bit shaken by what had happened. "What are we going to do with him if he is still alive?" she asked. Chen didn't need to think on this one. "I'll make him eat his produce and watch him suffer as Jia Li and Tan did. She suffered a quick but cruel death, so let him do the same. Lan Mei could see the hurt in his eyes; perhaps this would be the letting go of Jia Li.

Several hours had passed before they went to check on their unwelcome visitor. He was squirming around trying to free himself. The blow to the head just stunned him, but he was still bleeding. How he would have wished he had died from the blow, when he learned what was coming next, thought Chen. They left him to his pain and closed the door.

As dusk fell, they could hear the man calling out to them. So, Chen went to him. "Please I need some water," he pleaded. "Just a minute. I have something special for you," Chen told him as he walked away to fetch the basket. "I have some health food you are going to eat." They both watched to see his reaction, a look of terror suddenly appeared along with tears, and a plea of remorse. "You sold your health food to my partner and your own brother, and they both died of poisoning, so now it is your turn. If it is good enough for others, then it is good enough for you." All the colour drained from the man's face, he went ashen and the trembling started. He knew what lay ahead and it was far from a pleasant thought. "Don't make me eat that?" he pleaded. "Why?" asked Chen. Did he have enough guts to come clean or was his allegiance to the company above all else? Was he a man or a mouse? He turned out to be a mouse, and he would tell all to save his own life. "That food has been laced with arsenic; it causes a quick death." "That's good because you are going to have that experience my friend. You took my soulmate and my friend from me, so now I am going to take you away from your company. Not that you will be missed, but I missed my girlfriend so much. Your time has come to suffer as others have." He unwrapped the food and walked over to the man, who was pleading for his life, but it was too late. He clenched his jaw closed. Chen asked Lan Mei to help prise it open and he stuffed as much in as he could, then held his mouth closed. He had two choices, either choke to death or start eating and suffer the consequences. They knew if they let him live there would be only one survivor and it wouldn't be them. It was not nice to see the pain one went through as the arsenic worked its way through the body. They left before he took his final breath. There was no remorse from Chen, but Lan Mei was saddened by what she saw.

In the darkness of the night Chen and Lan Mei tied the wrapped body to the bar on Chen's bike. His legs were tied together and now that they had gone stiff, they were easier to tie to the bar. He kissed Lan Mei goodbye, then climbed on his bike with his legs astride the body and off he pedalled. He was heading for the cliff-top; it would take him two hours of pedalling to get there in the dark. Because he didn't want to draw unwanted attention, he carried a little hand-held torch which he shone on the road to see where he was going. He arrived at the cliff-top exhausted but without any incidents. He let his bike fall to the ground, as it was easier for him to cut the rope and drag the body over to the cliff edge, then he kicked it over the edge with his feet. His disgust for this man hopefully would disappear with the body. After disposing of the body, he cycled back home, as daybreak was appearing and Lan Mei was waiting for him.

China was now relaxing its lockdown procedures, as there was a reduction in the number of people contracting the virus. This did not include overseas travel as no countries were allowing visitors to enter. Chen had a desire to go to the country that the Nobel Prize winner, 'Mr X', lived, so he could meet him and exchange information. He wanted to share what he knew as he had proof of where the virus started. Well, not actual proof, as no-one was going to admit to anything, but he was so sure his findings were the truth.

Today Chen and Lan Mei decided to gather more evidence by visiting different neighbourhoods and asking people if their neighbours still lived there, or if they had moved on or died. Lan Mei took an area away from the condemned land just to see whether they had been affected as much as those closer to the shut-down area. She spent a full day enquiring and was shocked to find the high numbers of deaths that had occurred. The virus had gone from one family to the next as the people all mixed in supermarkets, schools, gyms and places of worship – that was until lockdown and social distancing came into play. This had certainly helped, as people became more aware of how contagious the virus had become, but now it was classed as a pandemic so they stayed indoors and isolated themselves and their families. Chen chose to visit nearer the disaster area, and he knew the results were going to be disheartening as they had seen the abandoned homes many times. Most of the company workers lived in close proximity to work. As he was cycling home, he was aware of a car following him so he pedalled down a narrow lane, but when he reached the end, there was the car waiting for him and two men got out. Knowing he couldn't escape, he dismounted and stood still. "What are you doing sniffing around this area?" asked one of the men. Chen had to think quick, so he told them he was looking to buy a house. "I've seen you in this area several times poking around. Are you searching for something?" Chen wondered who they were so politely asked them.

They said they were government officials checking up on the closed-off land site, and they didn't like unwanted attention drawn to the area, so told him to get on his bike and leave. This he thought was strange; it was like a warning, stay away or else!

He climbed on his bike and cycled to his house, and as he neared it, he slowed down, but he was not alone, as the car was still following him so he rode on past. He didn't want them to know where he lived. He cycled for half an hour then stopped at a café and bought a drink and sat outside where he could see them. After fifteen minutes they took off, so then he knew it was safe to cycle to his house without being followed, but just to make sure, he rode down narrow streets, taking the long way. Lan Mei was worried as the day was nearing an end and Chen hadn't come home. She was relieved to see him. He told her about his encounter with the two men. "It is almost as if they don't want anyone near the closed-off area. Do you think they are worried?" he asked her. After having tea, they sat and talked about their findings and were sad at the number of deaths that the virus had caused in such a small area.

That night as Lan Mei climbed into bed, she thought she heard a noise outside her bedroom window so crept through to Chen's room and climbed into his bed and snuggled into him. This was unexpected, so he lay still, and she felt warm and he could feel her body contours as she snuggled closer to him. He waited to see what was going to happen next, if she made a move of a sexual nature, then he would respond. His heart was beating fast, his body was responding to her closeness, he was aroused. Could he wait or was his body telling him it was time for him to make a move? With this he felt her hand moving down his spine, down his buttocks until it was nearing his throbbing organ. It was just too much; he turned over and pulled her hard to him. He wanted her right now in this moment so he guided his manly part to her body then entered. She wriggled around, pulling him further into her. She wanted all he could offer, they thrashed around together, delighting in each other. This was frenzied love making, nothing planned, just spur of the moment action, but with it came excitement. Neither had much time to think about things and nature just took its course, bringing with it an explosive passion.

This is how they found themselves the next morning, entwined in each other's arms, amid tangled bedclothes. Lan Mei was holding Chen's hand, which she lay across her breast wanting him to caress her. She was still in a loving mood, and she felt normal lying in bed next to him, while no disabilities were visible, making her feel like a complete woman. Love making made her feel beautiful within herself; it was one time when she felt she was no different to any other woman.

As the next morning progressed Lan Mei went back to her bedroom and pulled the drapes. It was then she saw an envelope stuck to the outside of her window. So, I did hear someone last night; I wasn't imagining it, she thought to herself. She unlocked the door and went to fetch the envelope, wondering who put it there and why! Inside was a folded note and after reading it, she called to Chen, who immediately appeared, thinking something was wrong. Just the look on her face told him she was upset. She handed him the note and on reading it he was angry, "Where did you find this?" She told him it was stuck on her window. "That is why I came to your bed last night. I thought I heard someone outside, and I was frightened. But who would know the salesman had been here? Someone must have missed him when he never returned home. "Oh Chen, what do we do now?" she sobbed. "We must keep calm and try to work through this. No doubt we will hear from them again. We will try to piece this together; perhaps we have missed something. Let us have breakfast and remember the fun we had last night. I'm disappointed to learn you only came to my bed because you were frightened," he told her jokingly. Lan Mei put her arms around him. "I've waited for this moment, but I had to be sure you were over Jia Li, and last night just seemed the right time for this to happen. Thank you, Chen, for making me feel like a woman. It has been sad for me with my disability. I still have sexual feelings, and I need to be loved, so it gives me back my self-belief once again." Chen felt sad to hear this is what she thought about herself, as inside she was a beautiful warm person. Next time they made love he would tell her this.

After breakfast Chen walked around the outside of the house to see if anything had been disturbed. He noticed footprints in the soil outside Lan Mei's window. He wondered who they belonged to and why the envelope had been stuck to her bedroom window, not that anyone would know who slept where! He had told Lan Mei to keep calm, but he himself felt far from calm. Did someone know the salesman's life had ended here, in this very house? That afternoon Chen put all his notes and cut-outs on the table, as he wanted to go through them. Did the letter from Mr X that circulated underground have a phone number or an e-mail address? Perhaps not, as he wouldn't want his private details out there, but he did remember what country he was from and that he was a Nobel Prize winner. From here he might be able to piece things together, if only he could make contact with him. They both had the same thoughts and proof of sorts, on how and where the virus began. He knew this was dangerous territory, as someone out there suspected something.

Chen and Lan Mei went to the library with the intention of looking through magazines that might disclose the identity of Mr X. They asked at the front desk where they would find information on past and present Nobel Prize winners, to which they were shown a section where they were all listed. They spent three hours searching, before Chen came across someone who he thought could be Mr X. It stated the country where he resided and as he continued to read, it mentioned he had worked in a pharmaceutical company in China. He was a professor of medicine, so he would definitely know all about the spread of viruses. Yes, this was his man. He had to make contact with him! He noted under the article a web address; perhaps this might be a start.

As he had no computer or any experience with computers he had to rely on Lan Mei. She wrote down the web address and they went to the library's computer room. As Lan Mei started up the computer Chen drafted out what he wanted her to type. She used her old work address as it was registered and she knew the password so if a reply came back, she could log in to it. Because the pharmaceutical company had closed down, she was sure no one would be using it. But was this in fact the case? The message Chen wanted to send read: *'I would like to make contact with you regarding the virus. I worked for the pharmaceutical company you mentioned in your report.'* He felt this was sufficient for a start; he didn't sign his name, as this would come later. Now all they could do was wait to see if Mr X was indeed interested enough to answer. They left the library feeling pleased that they had taken the time to do some research. Hopefully there would be contact made between the two parties.

Several days went by without any mishaps, but late one night there was a knock at their door. Chen went and opened it only to be pushed aside by two men who entered without an invitation. He immediately recognised them from the car incident several weeks back. "We are missing a salesman. He was last known to be coming to visit you, so what have you done to him?" bellowed one of the men. Chen told them no salesman had come to their house. "What was he selling?" he asked. The men looked at each other, neither wanting to admit to what the salesman was selling; they were not prepared to be questioned. Chen knew then they were part of the 'establishment'. They searched the house but found nothing so their departing words were "We will be watching you." Lan Mei hid behind the door when the men entered, and she knew where the hammer was if needed. They were both shaken by this intrusion. "What do you think they know?" she asked. "They are part of the 'establishment' and perhaps they know something through Tan's brother. They know we are on to them, and that's why they tried to poison us. Tomorrow we will buy a gun so we can protect ourselves if necessary.

The next morning as they were about to leave the house the phone rang. Chen answered it. "Mr X speaking. Your e-mail tells me we are both adamant on the same subject. You worked for the pharmaceutical company. Have you tried to make contact with any of the workers?" he asked. "Yes, we have, only three people have survived that we know of, my partner and I and another man, but he has since been poisoned by the company." "You must protect yourselves as they won't let up on you. They will try to take you out. I will arrange a safe passage out of China for you both as I have contacts. You must leave the country and if you don't, death is imminent! I will be in touch as soon as possible. Stay safe." After this conversation, they both knew their lives were in danger, as his words suggested he was an astute man.

This alerted Chen and Lan Mei to the need to hide their information, in such a place no-one would think to search. After deliberating for several hours, Lan Mei went to the spare bedroom with a pair of scissors and cut a slit in the bottom of the mattress. "Chen, put all your paperwork in here and I will stitch it up again." This they did, as it was inevitable their home would be searched again.

Today Chen wanted to go to the shop to pick up a weekend paper to see what was happening around the world. He checked the street before he left on his bike, just to make sure Lan Mei would be safe, then off he cycled. Lan Mei was busy about the house when she heard the door open. She called out to Chen, but instead the two men who had visited previously barged through. She was petrified. One came up to her and grabbed her by the arm. "Where is the computer?" he bellowed. The other man began searching, tossing everything on the floor. "We don't have a computer," she replied. "You have been using the company's website and their password. We know it's you, as no other workers are alive. You are the only one privy to the password. Who are you contacting?" he asked as he twisted her arm further, trying to get an answer from her, but Lan Mei would not budge. There was another sudden jerk of her arm, a bone snapped, followed by a loud scream. The guy let go. His search revealed nothing so they decided to leave with the following words, "We will be back." Lan Mei sat down in a chair nursing her arm, which she knew was broken as the pain was unbearable. She prayed that Chen was on his way home as she needed to see a doctor. Chen almost heard Lan Mei's plea for help, and suddenly he felt something was wrong so he cycled home flat out. He dropped his bike at the back door and was surprised to see the door wide open as he had told her to lock it while he was out of the house.

As he entered, he could hear Lan Mei sobbing and found her sitting in a chair holding her arm. "What happened?" he asked. Then he noticed the house was a mess; things had been flung on the floor. She told him everything and he knelt down in front of her. "You are so brave, Lan Mei, that's what I love most about you. We must go to the hospital and get help. Mr X is right, we have to leave China before it is too late. I can't believe they tracked us as the ones using the company's password, but there it is in black and white, they confessed to the knowledge that we were the only ones alive. I will note all this. Our company is bad. Look how it has rewarded all its loyal workers, with a pay off by death! It was going to be a half-hour walk to the hospital, but there was no other way. They agreed if any questions were asked, as to how and why this happened, they would say it was a fall. The hospital staff treated Lan Mei with kindness as they put her arm in plaster and told her she was very brave. Chen agreed. But behind the scenes they were unsure how this break had occurred as it was such a clean break, almost like it had been pulled backwards. They hoped it wasn't her partner who was the cause! Chen took Lan Mei home and put her to bed, then he cleaned up the mess, strewn all over the floor.

Now that all the drama was dealt with, Chen settled down to reading his paper. The virus was mostly under control in China, Taiwan, Australia and New Zealand, but it was a much darker picture elsewhere, especially in America, Europe and Britain, with many new deaths each day. It was likened to reading a horror story, and to think it started right here in his home town by his own company. The world was oblivious to the truth, but one day they would know, providing they weren't taken out before they left the country. As he perused the paper, he found a little article tucked away near the bottom of the page that took his eye. An enquiry into a missing salesman. The middle-aged man was known to be going to a particular area but never returned home that night. Did anyone know what had happened to him; if so, there was a handsome reward for any information leading to his whereabouts.' This sent a chill down Chen's spine. The 'establishment' knew exactly where he was going and what mission he was sent to carry out. All the suspicion was centred on the two of them – they were in deep trouble!

9

MR X'S PLANS

THE LONG-AWAITED phone call from Mr X had arrived! When Chen told him what had happened to Lan Mei, he was not surprised. Now that the 'establishment' knew they had used the company's password, Lan Mei would have to be gotten rid of. If no-one else from the company was alive, the two of them had to be dealt to. "I need you both to help me expose where and how the virus originated. I have tried, but without evidence I am not believed. To have two former employees from the actual pharmaceutical company, then it becomes real. I have good news: in two days' time a lady named 'Toshi' will call and pick you up in a white Toyota. Be ready as she will take you to a secret location where you will spend three nights. This is the start of your journey to a new life in a new country. I will tell you no more at the moment, other than you will receive instructions and each one will begin with the word 'Mr X.' If this is not used, then they are not my people. Be vigilant and stay safe, until we meet."

Chen and Lan Mei were taken by surprise. Only two more days left at their present address, then their life in China was nearing an end. They were not sad about this, as they knew the danger that awaited them if they didn't leave. It was only a matter of surviving the next two days! Chen had to work out what they were going to take with them. The house would be left as is, so as not to draw unwanted attention. A backpack each was what was agreed upon. Because both their parents, along with Chen's wife and Jia Li, were buried in mass graves, there was no special place to visit, so to leave the country was not a hard decision. All the sadness would be left behind and a new life awaited them.

They set out in piles what clothes were needed; they would leave Chen's notes and cuttings hidden until the morning they were leaving, as there was still one night to go. Excitement mixed with fear made them decide on an early night. Their clothes were sitting by their backpacks ready to be packed in the morning. As they cuddled up in bed, Lan Mei felt relaxed and playful so began seducing Chen. This would be their last love-making session in this bed, but his mind was elsewhere. He was far from relaxed; he was on edge so his body would not respond to her touching. Suddenly they heard noises outside: someone was banging on their door. Chen told Lan Mei to hide behind the bedroom door, while he went to see what was happening. He pondered whether to open the door, but he realised they would break it down if he didn't, so he unlocked it. In stormed the two men who had visited several times. They grabbed him and dragged him through the house. Then one of them spotted the backpacks and the pile of clothes, "Going somewhere I see. Well, no, the only place you two are going is to your graves." They threw Chen to the floor. His mind was in overdrive: what could he do? He reached out and pulled one of the men off balance and he fell to the ground. At that moment Lan Mei appeared from behind and hit the standing man over the head with the hammer then threw the hammer to Chen who clobbered the guy on the floor. It was then they realised this was meant to be the end for them both. Instead, the perpetrators were going to be the ones who would never take another breath. There was a moan from the man who Lan Mei hit. "What will we do with him?" she asked. "We will finish him off. It is us or them," and he picked up the hammer and did the deed. There was no worry with the other guy as his skull was smashed in; he was well dead. Lan Mei could not believe no tears were forthcoming when confronted with this grizzly murder scene, and all her emotions were put aside as she took in what Chen said: it's them or us.

What were they going to do with the bodies? They couldn't dispose of them, so instead they put a cover over them. It didn't matter any more as they would be gone tomorrow. No-one would know where they were. Well, not for a couple of days they hoped, just enough time for them to get out of the country. Both their lives would have a hefty price tag on them now. There was no more sleep to be had, so they took the notes and papers from the mattress and packed them into their backpacks along with their clothes. Once this was finished, they sat on their bed wrapped in each other's arms and waited as the minutes ticked by. The minutes seemed to run into hours. They were petrified; who did these bodies lying dead on the floor belong to? They were part of the 'establishment', this much they knew. But no matter how much blame lay with them, Lan Mei was not an advocate of 'a life for a life'. She pleaded with Chen to leave a note saying this was in self-defence. "But Lan Mei it doesn't matter, no one is going to believe us; we are the enemy, we are dead in their eyes. Our strength has to be with ourselves. We are our own biggest worry at this moment."

They sat in silence then Lan Mei came up with an idea. "Why don't we set the house on fire then they will be burnt. When they find the bodies, they will think they belong to you and me?" "If we do that it will alert the authorities straight away. We have to get as far away as possible before the bodies are discovered," replied Chen. On second thoughts he wondered if this was the thing to do, as on finding the bodies the authorities would think they belonged to the occupants of the house, until they did a post-mortem, and by then they would have left China. They decided to set the thermostat on the heater to come on at 11pm when everyone was asleep, as this would give the house time to burn before drawing attention. They placed a blanket in front of the heater so it would catch fire.

Morning had dawned when the long-awaited knock finally arrived. Chen looked out the window and saw the white Toyota car; it was early but the best time to disappear before many neighbours were up and about. Chen went to the door and the first word spoken was "Mr X". Then Toshi introduced herself, so he asked her in while they picked up their bags. She saw something covered up on the floor and noticed the blood trickling from under the cover. "What happened?" she asked. Chen hurriedly explained. "Then let's get out of here quick. I will check to see no-one is around then I will signal for you to come to the car." They waited and when the coast was clear, the signal was given. Into the car they climbed. Lan Mei struggled to get in with her broken arm, but every minute was precious. It was only when they drove out of their street that Chen felt a little more relaxed. They were on their way, only just in one piece!

Toshi told them they would drive all day and through the night so they would get to their destination before the morning traffic built up. They stopped at lunchtime to have a bite to eat and use the bathroom then they were on their way again. On a quiet piece of the road, she stopped and changed the car number plates. "What did you do that for?" Chen asked. "If anyone saw me leave your house and they took the plate numbers, we will not be followed, as they no longer belong to us." He thought this was very smart, and he could see this was a professional outfit and this made him feel safe. She said that when they reach their destination, she would take a separate photo of them so as to arrange a passport and visa for them to enter their new country. "I have arranged an apartment in Pudong, the business centre of Shanghai, for you for three nights.

You will be safe there, as millions of people work there, and it is the place to go to get lost among the crowds. Just keep to yourselves, go sightseeing but try not to speak to people. I have stocked the fridge with food so you don't have to go to the food stalls. Mr X has opened a bank account for you in your new country and I will give you money for your stay in Pudong. Remember the password if you have anyone knocking at your door; do not open it if the password is not used. The hotel is very secure as we use it often. If you think of any questions before we get there, just ask." They stopped at a café to eat once more, then they were on the road again. The roads were busy as night was approaching, with people out and about. Then about midnight the traffic died down on the motorway so they were able to gain more speed. Toshi hoped they would make the apartment before the busy morning traffic blocked the streets in Shanghai, as they were heading to the other side of the city. "You must take a ride on the MagLev from the station to the airport, a distance of 30 kilometres by road, but seven minutes on the fast train. It is a wonderful experience," she told them.

On arriving at their apartment both Chen and Lan Mei were exhausted. They had just made it before the early morning traffic built up, but Toshi was used to the busy roads as she had done this many times. Her company was employed to supply a safe passage to people who needed to leave the country unnoticed; in other words, under cover! She took the necessary photos for the passports and said she would be back in three days' time with all the papers that were needed to cross to their new country. They thanked her as she left, then they heard the door click closed, and now it was time to fall into bed and sleep.

It was mid-afternoon when Chen woke; Lan Mei was still asleep. The first thing on his mind was the fire: had his house burnt down and were the two bodies found? He was desperate to get a paper, as he had to know. He decided to go down to reception to buy one, but then thought better of it, as all they would have was the local paper, so he decided to have a shower. When he came back to the bedroom Lan Mei was up and dressed. The first thing she said was, "Chen, do you think your house has gone?" "We will go for a walk and find a paper from our region." As they passed through reception, Lan Mei picked up a couple of the hotel business cards, and she put one in Chen's pocket and one inside her bra. Once out on the street, there before them stood the beautiful Oriental Pearl Tower ,which created a picture of two dragons playing with pearls. They both knew of this famous landmark but to see it first hand was simply stunning! Lan Mei stood in wonder. "I have never seen anything so beautiful," she told Chen. But the only thing on his mind at this moment was finding a paper. They found a street vendor with a newspaper stand and sorted through until they found what they were looking for. Chen tucked it under his arm; he would not open it until they were in the privacy of their apartment. The streets were a constant throng of people rushing in all directions. They recognised the bridge they had passed over earlier in the morning. Toshi had told them Pudong was a man-made island, as there was nowhere to build a new business centre, so they created their own island. One had to cross the Huangpu River to get to Pudong, which was linked by two bridges and a river tunnel underpass. It had become a famous district in Shanghai, with skyscrapers aplenty. In fact, recently it had been announced that the land was gradually sinking with the weight of the many tall buildings.

The paper was burning a hole in Chen's arm as he desperately wanted to see if there was any reference to his house fire, so they started back, but the streets were now full of workers making their way home and it took them much longer to return. It was a relief to leave the hustle and bustle of the crowds and return to peace and quiet. They both settled at the table to peruse the paper. Nothing appeared on the front page, but the next page told a different story. There before them was an image of the ruins of Chen's house, under the headlines: 'Young couple perish as house burns to the ground'. 'Two bodies have been recovered and they are thought to be those of the occupants of the house. A post-mortem is being conducted to confirm this finding. The fire was thought to have started about midnight, but the house was almost demolished when the fire appliances arrived. Neighbours said the couple kept very much to themselves but were friendly.'

There was no regret felt by Chen, as for him it was the end of an era that had brought with it dread and fear. But for Lan Mei there was sadness, as it was where she had first made love to Chen, and it was her place of refuge after losing her parents to the virus. She loved living there, as Chen had given her back her self-respect, he made her feel like a complete woman again and this meant the world to her … it made her feel special. She shed a tear in remembrance.

Darkness was falling so Lan Mei prepared tea for them. They discussed over the meal what they would do the next day. Toshi had told them about the MagLev being the fastest train in the world, so they decided this was tomorrow's treat. As they pulled the curtains, the lights from the Oriental Pearl Tower lit up the sky like a Christmas tree; it was beautiful! Lan Mei asked Chen to hold her in his arms, and she felt serene and happy. While close to each other, a warm feeling flowed through Chen's veins, the urge to make love to her took over, so he picked her up and carried her to the bedroom and lay her on the bed. He undressed her, mindful of her broken arm, and then stripped off himself. The caressing started with both participating, then it turned into a frenzy, thus leading to an explosive union of two eager bodies who revelled in each other's joy. This is what Lan Mei longed for, this was the moment when she felt as an equal. She wished these moments would last forever, but when they happened, she felt blessed. They dropped off to sleep totally exhausted.

10

A FACE FROM THE PAST

TODAY IT WAS off to the train station for a ride on the amazing MagLev. Lan Mei found the hotel business card on the floor; it must have fallen from her bra the previous night when Chen undressed her, so she picked it up and tucked it back in her bra, which was the handiest place at this moment. They put on their face masks before walking to the station where there were crowds of people, all waiting to get on the train. Chen grabbed her hand as he went to jump aboard so as not to leave her behind. They searched until they found a seat where they could sit together. Within a few minutes they were floating on magnetised rails as the MagLev sped its way to the airport. The houses and fields swished past in a blink; it was exhilarating. When they reached the airport, they stayed on the train as they had bought return tickets. While it was stopped, Lan Mei noticed a man staring at her. She turned away then looked back again and there he was, his eyes fixed on her. She studied him for a moment, then suddenly realised that she knew him through work. He was a top scientist and it was obvious he remembered her… But she was meant to be dead, in fact burnt to death in a house fire. The 'establishment' had let him know this last night. Lan Mei was petrified; should she tell Chen? No, she decided against this as it would upset him; she would tell him tonight. As the train pulled into the station, the man jumped up and made his way towards Lan Mei. She stood up and told Chen to hurry, so they mingled with the crowds leaving the train. She kept her head down hoping to lose the man, but instead lost Chen.

Here she was alone at an overcrowded station, among thousands of people, feeling sad and inadequate, her disability dragging her down. She wanted to burst out crying but remembered Toshi's words: "Don't speak to anyone". This was when she had to pull herself together and be brave. Chen had told her that was what he loved most, her bravery. She looked around and spotted the man in a distance. He was still searching for her, so hurriedly she put her head down so as not to be recognised. Tears were welling up in her eyes. Where was Chen? She found a seat, so sat down in case he was looking for her. She would wait!

She closed her eyes to hide her tears, then she felt someone touching her shoulder. "Chen," she whispered, but on opening her eyes, there stood the scientist from her work. "What the hell are you doing here?" he said. "We thought you and your boyfriend had died in the house fire as two bodies were found. Who do the bodies belong to?"

Lan Mei froze for a minute, she had to think quick, she had to be brave, she had to get rid of him, and suddenly a thought came to her. She grabbed the man and as he tried to push her away, she screamed, "Help, Help! He is attacking me." From the outside this looked like an assault, so two guards came rushing to her rescue and handcuffed the man. "He tried to hurt me; I am a cripple!" she cried. She watched as he was led away and loaded into a police van, then driven off. Now it was time for her to escape. She started to make her way, but to where? She was lost. She stood for several minutes, then remembered she had the hotel business card in her bra. She was able to show people the card and they put her in the right direction.

Chen was frantic. He had lost Lan Mei. How would she manage without him? He walked up and down the station being pushed and shoved in all directions, but he had to find her. After half an hour he realised this search was fruitless, as there were millions of people in a small area. What should he do? Would she find her way back to the hotel? He decided to walk to the hotel and check to see if she was in fact there already.

Their apartment was empty; Lan Mei had not come back. He went down to the foyer and decided to wait there for her. As time ticked by, he became worried, put his head in his hands and prayed she would come back to him. Tears began to form. He couldn't imagine life without her. Had someone recognised her? He felt sick. "Hi, Chen. I lost you." He looked up and there was Lan Mei. He jumped up and ran to her. "Thank God you are safe!" "Please, Chen, I have something to tell you. Can we go to our apartment?"

She sat at the table and took Chen's hand. "Today I saw someone on the train I know from the company and he recognised me. He tried to get to me as we were alighting, that's why I asked you to hurry. I put my head down so I would lose him, and instead I lost you. I was sitting on a seat with my eyes closed when I felt a hand on my shoulder; it was him! He said to me, 'I thought you were burnt to death in a house fire. Two bodies were found and if they weren't yours, then who did they belong to?'" Chen jumped up in shock. "Lan Mei, he probably followed you here, now they will know where we are." "No, Chen I was brave." She told him what she had done and that he had been taken away in a police van. "Oh, how brave were you? You are so clever. How did you find your way back here?" She showed him the hotel business card. Chen was so proud of his girl, not only did she have a heart of gold, but she was clever and had a good brain and a big limp, which he never noticed any more.

After this episode they decided to spend their last day in the apartment. No, they had to find the street vendor and buy another paper to see if any more had eventuated from the fire. Off they went hand in hand; Chen wasn't about to lose her again! It didn't take long for them to find the vendor as he was standing on the pavement waving papers in his hand, "Read all about it … huge reward for missing couple … latest news … read all about it." This stopped Chen and Lan Mei in their tracks. He let her hand go and bought a paper. "Thank you, sir, read all about it," he yelled as he handed over the paper. There on the front page was another photo of the burnt-out house. My God, this was now headline news! Chen grabbed Lan Mei by the hand and they hurried back to the safety of their hotel. They would definitely not be leaving their room again today. Chen spread the paper out on the table and the front-page news read, 'The bodies found in the burnt-out ruins were not those of the occupants, as first thought. A post-mortem revealed the charred remains belonged to two unidentified men in their early sixties. Police are investigating as to the whereabouts of the house owners as they have not been seen since the fire. Anyone knowing of their whereabouts are asked to report to the police immediately. A large reward has been offered for any information.' Chen and Lan Mei looked at each other in shock. They had entered into the world of crime, as they were now classed as murder suspects. "The man who recognised you yesterday, he knows we are here in Pudong. I wonder if he will tell the police?" asked Chen. "The 'establishment' will know the two men, as they will not have come back from their mission to silence us. Our lives are in grave danger, as not only are the police looking for us, but the company will be out to get us at any cost as they know we can expose them. Only one more night in China … please let us be safe," Lan Mei whispered.

They lay about thinking of all the scenarios that confronted them. Not one was less complicated than the other. It was tonight Toshi would be bringing the papers and instructions for them, to cross the East China Sea to their new country ... to freedom! Most of the afternoon they spent dozing off. The pressure was building; it was only hours before they were to leave, but so many things could go wrong. At tea time they turned on the television to listen to the news, especially to see how the virus was panning out. Was the spread declining? They hoped this was the case. The first news item began as follows: 'The owners of the house where the two charred bodies were found have been seen in the business centre of Pudong. A man recognised them on the MagLev yesterday. They are a young couple, the girl has a disability. Please report to the police if you have any information.' The world was now closing in on them, and the closer they were getting to freedom, the more dangerous it was becoming.

As night-time fell, they waited anxiously for Toshi to knock on their door, but as the hours slipped by, that knock never eventuated. They went to bed at midnight frightened and confused. Had they been abandoned because of the newscast? At some ungodly hour of the morning Chen stirred. Someone was shaking him and he jumped up in fright to find Toshi leaning over him. "Chen, wake Lan Mei up and get dressed. We have to move quickly," she whispered. It was still dark. They dressed and put their clothes in their backpacks and went through to the lounge. "What is the time?" asked Lan Mei, rubbing her eyes. "It is 5.30am. We have to get to the ferry terminal before the rush of traffic begins. Besides, police are everywhere; we have to be extremely careful," replied Toshi. "Always wear your face masks."

At the terminal they were stopped by security, a

routine check they said. Toshi flashed her pass so they let her through. "I know most of the security guys; we look after them and they look after us. I have a small office in the terminal. You walk with me, Lan Mei, and you trail behind, Chen, as there will be police everywhere after last night's broadcast. They will be checking all passengers who are boarding the ferry, so we have a plan as to how to get you on. You are booked into cabin 14 for the two days it will take to reach Osaka. Once there, you will be met by Marcel who will put you on the night train to Nagoya. Remember the password, and don't go with anyone who doesn't use Mr X. Toshi gave them their last instructions along with their passports and visitors' visas. "Once you reach Japan you are safe. We want you to board the ferry separately; don't ever be seen together as the police will be checking young couples. Go to your cabin and only come out to get food. Just be mindful in case the police search your cabin. Find a place to hide one of the backpacks, and only have one on show. Be vigilant at all times. Good luck my friends. Mr X will look after you both." It was time for them to board the ferry; they hugged Toshi and said their final farewells.

Chen was the first on the ferry, then five minutes later Lan Mei made her way on board. He couldn't help looking back to see if she was coming, but he lost her in the crowds. He worried that she would be recognised because of her disability, not that she saw it like that. The police presence was truly overwhelming. They were checking all the couples as they came onto the ferry. Then he spotted Lan Mei, who was stopped by the police. They were talking to her, but he was sure she could handle herself; she was smart!

When asked to stop, Lan Mei had to inwardly hide her fear. She remembered Toshi's words, 'Act normal at all times', so this she would do. "Why are you going to Japan and for how long?" a police officer enquired. She told him she was going for her cousin's wedding and she intended staying for a month. "I see you are on your own. Can you manage without help?" he questioned her. "I have looked after myself for years and, yes, I am very independent. I don't need a keeper." He looked at her and wondered what she meant by that? Perhaps she had taken what he said in the wrong context. Suddenly he was called away by his comrade so didn't have time to apologise. He yelled to her, "I will see you later." Poor Lan Mei, what was she meant to do? Perhaps if she was seen in police company, she would be protected. "What a funny young lady!" the police officer said to his comrade. Her steps quickened as she lost sight of the officers. Panic had set in and she had to get to her cabin: only then would she feel safe. The ferry was packed with people crossing the ocean to get home to Japan. Surely, she wouldn't run into that officer again – not on this packed ferry.

Once together again Lan Mei felt safe. She needed Chen; he was her strength. They lay on their bed and rested. It had been a stressful day for them both but now it was nearly over. Chen was feeling more excited, as he couldn't wait to meet Mr X. They had so much to discuss, and together they had the power to expose the source of the virus. He knew it wouldn't be without its pitfalls but he was ready. Mr X had the brains and connections. Together they had the proof; it was a good combination. They had no idea where or when they were going to meet him, but first they had to make it to Japan.

When it was time to eat, Chen decided to go first, then he could tell Lan Mei where to go. It wasn't long before he was back, and now it was her turn. "Be careful on deck as the sea is quite rough. Hold on to the rails," he instructed her. As she was making her way along the deck the ferry started rolling and although she held onto the rail, a sudden thump lurched her forwards, she lost her grip on the rail and fell to the deck. She lay there and people started gathering, some offering to help her. "Please move on everyone," and there was the officer she had spoken to earlier. He helped her up so she could grab on to the rail. Lan Mei thanked him and started to walk away. "Excuse me miss, did I offend you earlier?" "I'm fine, people see a disability and think we should have a full-time career. That is not the case, and we like to think of ourselves as independent and able, in fact normal," she replied. Then she thought for a moment, "Why are there so many police on this ferry, is this normal?" "No, we are on the lookout for a couple who are thought to be fleeing the country," he replied. Could she be a little cheekier, "What have they done?" she asked. "It's all over the news, their house burnt down and two charred bodies were found in the ruins. The post-mortem revealed the bodies were not those of the house owner and his partner. The government want them detained in China, so they have offered a large reward. All passages out of China have a heavy police presence." With this she thanked him once again and made her way to the café. But the thought of what she had just heard had curbed her appetite. She had to get back to Chen, so made do with a coffee and a sandwich.

When she came back to the cabin, Chen was waiting, as he thought something had happened to her. She told him about her encounter with the officer and what conversation had transpired. "The powers that be are definitely worried; no wonder a large sum has been put on our heads. Everyone will be looking for us, civilians included," added Chen. Then he remembered that Toshi had said to only have one backpack visible at all times, in case of a cabin search. They hid the spare backpack under the pillows on the bed.

Chen had a look through the onboard compendium to see if there was a lounge with a television as he was keen to see the day's news, and yes there was. He told Lan Mei he was going to listen to the news and for her to stay in the cabin, as she always seems to attract unwanted attention. He wasn't sure if it was her disability and people felt sorry for her, but they needn't! As he made his way to the lounge, he couldn't get over the police presence on the deck and at the entrance to the lounge. All the seats were taken so he stood at the back of the room. People were talking and he picked up on little bits and pieces of conversations, the topic being the young couple wanted for arson and murder. It was only a few minutes to the next news cast, and he awaited with bated breath: what was he going to hear? Then it began; 'Breaking News … 'The two charred remains from the house fire have been formally identified and were believed to have been connected to a pharmaceutical company that had closed down. It was situated next to the Xihun market. The government have tripled the reward money, hoping the public will get on board and help detain this couple. They are believed to be trying to leave the country. They were last seen on the MagLev in Pudong last week, by a man who recognised the young lady and went to approach her. She pretended he was attacking her, so unfortunately the attention was diverted to him, allowing her to escape. We are appealing to all citizens to help the police find this couple.' Poor Chen, he had heard enough. Thank God they were wearing masks as they were a partial disguise, although no images had been posted. Only one more day and it would all be over!

As he returned to the cabin, he knocked on the door and gave the password. Lan Mei opened the door, but before he could tell her what he had heard, she burst out, "Chen, the police knocked on the door and demanded it to be opened, then they searched the cabin to check there was no-one else here. Thank goodness Toshi told us to hide one of our backpacks, and that you had left the cabin." When Chen told her what the news revealed, the colour drained from her face. "Do you think they are on to us?" He reassured her that they had no idea where they were. "You know Lan Mei, the government is desperate to find us before we leave the country. They are worried they will be exposed, and that is why they have increased the reward. They want every man, woman and child out there looking for us, they want us silenced." It was bedtime so they cuddled up and drifted off to sleep, exhausted mentally.

All that was left for them to do was to survive another day and night at sea. It was decided Chen would get the food and Lan Mei would stay in the cabin. It was going to be a long twenty-four hours, but she knew of an enjoyable way to pass the time. Chen went in search of food, but he had to be careful not to look as if he was buying for two people, so they would be on rations for the next few meals. The morning passed slowly so after lunch Lan Mei suggested they go back to bed. She wanted to feel that complete woman again, the one that was just like anyone else. The caressing started, she ran her hands down Chen's thighs, tickling and gently pinching him, then moving her hands around to his genitals, where she played with him, arousing his sexual feelings. Then she lay back while he kissed and caressed her. She loved him touching her and smothering her with kisses, and her body started arching with pleasure. She needed him to become part of her, so she pulled him tightly to her until they became as one. This was the moment she felt beautiful and complete. Nothing could take this feeling from her; it was her moment in life to be equal to every other woman.

When they woke it was dark; they had slept the whole afternoon, but now it was time to eat again. Chen had a shower and dressed to go and get some food, as they had worked up an appetite. He came back and they shared what he bought; it wasn't much but tomorrow things would be entirely different. All that was left was to have a good night's sleep and be prepared for their first day of freedom. That was easier said than done! They talked about what was to happen when they left the ferry, they were going to be met by Marcel who would put them on the night train from Osaka to Nagoya. If the ferry arrived on schedule, they had three hours before catching the train. They knew they had to leave the ferry separately and that Marcel would be waiting on the dock with a place with an 'X' on it. Chen was to be the first to leave, and he would find Marcel then they would look for Lan Mei, who was to walk behind them to the waiting vehicle. This was an extra safety precaution. Once whisked away from the ferry terminal, their worries would be all but over. They went over these plans several times so there would be no slip-ups. It was going to be chaos as they alighted from the ferry, with hundreds of other passengers returning home, but all was sorted in their minds!

They were woken by the ferry's horn as it neared the dock, which was to let the passengers know it was time to pack up and get ready to disembark. Now the adrenalin was starting to kick in; it was only a couple more hours to freedom. The last hurdle was to get off the ferry without being recognised. Chen decided it was better for them to skip breakfast, as the less contact with the outside world the safer he felt. His main worry was Lan Mei: her disability was something that couldn't be disguised, not that any images had been posted yet. In his own mind they were ninety-nine per cent safe; however, there was that one little shadow of doubt.

Chen decided to go out on deck and watch the ferry dock, so he kissed Lan Mei goodbye. The next time they would meet officially would be in Marcel's vehicle. He gave her a reassuring smile as he opened the cabin door. After he left, she sat on the bed and mentally went over the sequences of events that were about to happen. She did a quick meditation to bring her mind to a good place and when she felt calm, she stood up ready to go. She put on a floppy hat, picked up the backpack and made for the door. Lan Mei took a deep breath before putting on her mask, then made her way along the deck, making sure she had a good grip on the rail, as she didn't want to slip and draw unwanted attention to herself. Little did she know there was an image of herself, right at that moment, flashing over the news. She put her head down and took her time, as the slower she walked the less noticeable her bung leg became. Just as she was nearing the gangway, she felt a tap on her shoulder. She looked around and there was the officer that she had encountered several times on the journey. "I am here to escort you; we can't have you falling again. Do you have anyone meeting you when you leave the ferry?" he asked. He felt for this young lady; she disregarded her disability and got on with life, and she was a brave soul who intrigued him in more ways than one. He would remember her! "I can manage without help, thank you. You are most kind," she replied. "What about friends, are they going to meet you?" he asked. "I have a car waiting to take me to where I need to go. Nice to have met you – goodbye," and she walked off towards the disembarkation area. She took out her passport, ready to have it stamped. The ticket box was surrounded by police who were checking all passengers as they left; this was the last point that they could make an arrest. From here on the responsibility lay with Japan's government.

The officers eyed Lan Mei up and down, as here was a young lady with a disability, but she seemed to be on her own. "Did you come aboard with anyone?" they asked. She told them she was travelling alone, as she was going to a cousin's wedding. "Right, off you go!" she was told. She couldn't wait to leave behind the ferry and the police officers that accompanied it. Now to find Chen and Marcel. She walked through the terminal looking as she went, but there was no sign of them. It was a nightmare trying to find anyone in this crowd, she thought to herself. As she was standing waiting, a young girl came up to her and asked if she the lady was on television. Lan Mei was startled, "What do you mean?" she asked. "I saw a picture of a lady. She lit a fire. Are you her?" This threw her into a panic; was her image in fact on television? She began to perspire. "No, that's not me." She pulled her hat down further so her eyes were covered as fear had taken over. Would someone else recognise her before she reached safety. She noticed the young girl was tugging at her mother's dress and pointing her way. This was a signal to disappear quickly so she walked to the other end of the terminal. It was there she saw Chen, who waved, and she knew to follow him. Lan Mei was relieved; she hoped she didn't have to walk far as she felt mentally exhausted.

The man with Chen must be Marcel, she thought. When they reached the car, Chen opened the back door for her to climb in, then the introductions were made. She couldn't hide her tears; they flowed uncontrollably. "Chen, did you know my image is on the news?" Marcel interrupted and told them he had just seen the latest news update from China and yes, Lan Mei's image was there for everyone to see. Their nightmare was over, thank God. Marcel assured them they were safe in Japan. "But it will be good to get you away from Osaka, and once in Nagoya you will just be part of millions of people in Tokyo. Because Osaka is the main entry port from China, they often have China's news, but in Nagoya it will be Japanese news.

Meanwhile back on the ferry, the police were called into a meeting as an image had just been released of the 'wanted' young lady. The kind officer knew immediately who she was. He had missed the chance to arrest her and claim the huge reward; if only he had seen this sooner. But then he thought of her bad leg and what a brave soul she was, so perhaps he would say nothing and give her a chance. She stirred a feeling of pity within his heart.

Marcel told them they would drive straight to the train station as the roads were getting busy and he didn't want them to be late. They were to be on the overnight train and Mr X would be there to meet them at the other end. The train would arrive at Nagoya station at 10am. Chen asked Marcel, "Have you met Mr X?" "No, I work for Toshi's company, and we are contracted to deliver people safely; that's what we are paid to do." "Do you know anything about him?" Chen asked. Marcel said he knew of him. He was a controversial figure, in fact a Nobel Prize recipient but a brilliant man apparently.

Marcel encountered no problems with the traffic, so they had a straight run through to the train station, leaving them an hour before the train was due to leave. Chen suggested they looked for some food as he was famished. It was time to get something into their bellies after half starving themselves on the ferry. He asked Marcel to join them, but he declined as he had another pick-up to do. "Our company helps to get people out of China for various reasons. Toshi owns the company, and she has contacts in most countries, so we are kept busy. I will arrange your tickets while you find somewhere to eat." It didn't take long for him to return with everything in order. "Here are your tickets. Be in the queue fifteen minutes before the train leaves. Good luck guys," he called to them, then he was gone. They found a café with a variety of food so ordered plenty to make up for the shared meals on the ferry. Suddenly their appetite had returned, their bodies felt lighter as they had rid themselves of a heavy load, consisting of stress and China. "Oh, to feel free, it seems such a long time since this all started," sighed Lan Mei. Then she fell silent, remembering their families and work colleagues who had died. Was it wrong for them to feel happy in a time of such sadness? But she reminded herself that they too had suffered along the way, but now they were going to prove where this virus started and one day the truth would be revealed.

They were on the train. Marcel had booked them into

a carriage that had sleeping compartments, in which the beds pulled down when they were ready to be used. They sat and talked non-stop, their excitement mounting. Chen was so wanting to meet Mr X. What would he be like? Where were they going to live? He had promised to look after them in exchange for information that would turn the world upside down. Their future had not been talked about much, as they didn't know what it held for them, but now it was all they had!

As the train pulled into Nagoya station it was bang on time. They tidied themselves as they wanted to look presentable to meet Mr X. He was an intelligent man, so they wanted him to like them. On went their backpacks then they made their way onto the platform. The station was busy, and they didn't know where they had to meet, so they found a seat and sat down to gather their thoughts. Only a few minutes passed before a voice interrupted them. "Hello Chen, it is Chen? I'm pleased to meet you, I'm Mr X but, in reality, Mr Yamakawa. At long last we meet," and he bowed to Chen. Chen introduced Lan Mei and he bowed to her. An immediate feeling of warmth flowed between them. "I know things have been difficult for you both as I have been following your progress; Toshi has kept me up to date. Now that your life is going down a new path, I know you will be happy. I am looking forward to working with you both. This project has taken over my life. I know what I have uncovered is true, but I didn't have the actual proof, but now I have you. Forgive me, we will get you settled, then we can talk business." Both Chen and Lan Mei found Mr Yamakawa to be a charming man, so polite, but as they would discover this was Japanese custom. "I'm so happy we made it here in one piece and together. So many unpleasant incidents have happened. We have been responsible for the death of three men, all who were trying to silence us and all from the 'establishment'. We were a threat to them, being among the very few who survived. But from the moment I read your article I wanted to meet you, because I know it revealed the truth," Chen said in all sincerity. In this moment there was a bond formed that would develop into a partnership of profound significance for the rest of the world.

Mr Yamakawa drove them into the heart of the city where he owned a house that was to be their home. They were amazed how different Japan was to China. They didn't see any slum areas and everything seemed orderly and tidy. Although the houses were close together, they all had little gardens. Occasionally Lan Mei spotted tiny dwarfed trees which Mr Yamakawa explained were bonsai, the raising and pruning of which was a common hobby in Japan. Lan Mei laughed at these funny plants, as she had never seen them before. She felt happy at the thought of perhaps growing her own one day. The car came to a stop outside a tidy little house. "Come, this is your home. It is fully furnished and all you have to buy is food. I have stocked your fridge with the necessities" He took them inside and explained how everything worked. It was like a little doll's house; there was Japanese art on the wall and origami decorations hanging from the ceiling. Screens separated one room from the next. This was so foreign to them both, but they were delighted with their little house. "I have opened a bank account in your name, all the details and papers are on the table, along with an envelope with enough yen to get you started. I will leave you to settle in for a couple of days, then I will come back," he said as he bowed to them. As they thanked him, they found themselves returning his bows. "What a lovely culture; they are so polite, Chen, I love it here already," stated Lan Mei.

The two days passed so quickly, as they had been for walks to familiarise themselves with their new surroundings. Each person they passed and spoke to bowed to them so they returned the bows. Most of the elderly didn't speak English so they smiled instead. Lan Mei spent a lot of time in her garden admiring the plants. Chen, on the other hand, was sorting through his papers and cuttings, as he wanted it all in order for Mr Yamakawa when he was next in touch, which was meant to be today! After they had lunch, a car pulled up outside on the street and after a few minutes Mr Yamakawa came down the path. He was a well-dressed man, small in stature, but who looked very business-like and wore very thick glasses. Chen opened the door and invited him in, and he did his customary bow. "Are you all settled in – do you need anything?" he asked. They let him know they were very happy and, no, they had everything they needed. "My office is only two blocks away. I will take you there in my car and you can walk back, so you know how to get there tomorrow." They drove to his office and he pointed out which alleyway to take to his office. "This is where we will do our business. It has to be kept confidential; I am a very private person so there won't be many interruptions. As I have mentioned, this virus has taken over my life, and I have to prove this is a manufactured virus. Without your input I can't go much further, so together we will make the world sit up and take notice. One country alone does not have the right to take so many lives; people must know where it started and by whom. I am a professor of medicine so am well versed with how viruses spread and what can cause them. I shouldn't bore you with this now, but if you come to my office tomorrow morning at 8am, we will get down to business." Mr Yamakawa got out of his car and came around to open the doors for them to climb out, followed by a bow. They said their goodbyes and parted.

11

DOWN TO BUSINESS

TODAY WAS the day Chen had been waiting for. He was going to be working alongside his mentor on a subject dear to both their hearts. He was sure he and Lan Mei were going to learn many things that would sometimes be beyond their comprehension, but they were up for it, and they had come this far, so they were not going to give up now! They would not have been murderers had it not been to save their own lives. Lan Mei organised breakfast while Chen gathered up his notes and papers and put them in his backpack. It would only take them ten minutes to walk to the office, as they had timed themselves yesterday.

At 7.45am they were knocking on Mr Yamakawa's office door, as Chen wanted to be early and he was itching to get started on the subject of the virus. As they entered his office, they were astounded by the size of the bookcases that reached the ceiling and were jammed full of books, as well as diagrams of countries and animals hanging on the walls. This was definitely a professor's paradise. He greeted them with a bow and asked them to sit down. "Now my children, I will tell you what I know then we will get down to business. I have done 40 years' research on animals and viruses so I know this is not a natural virus. I worked for four years at the Xihun laboratory so knew many of the people who worked there. When the virus outbreak was made public, I tried to contact some of my former colleagues but their phones were dead. It wasn't until a few weeks later a friend of mine who was working near the laboratory told me most of the workers had died. This was when I became suspicious. This is where you two come in, as you both worked first-hand for the company. How you managed to survive is a miracle! This is likened to World War 3, only instead of countries fighting, a silent killer had been released, to make it look as if the blame lay with no-one. China has to be exposed and made accountable for this despicable act. There were rumours it was formulated in Harvard University in America before it was stolen by China, perhaps this is why there is such animosity between these two superpowers. America is certainly not going to admit to any of this. I have put that theory aside, whether true or false, but the blame lies with China, as it was the country that released the virus. I have no proof of how it was spread, but this is where you may be able to help me."

Chen couldn't wait to tell the professor what he and Lan Mei had discovered. Where to start was the problem.

He decided to start at the beginning when he first became suspicious that something sinister was happening. He lost his wife and parents to what was diagnosed as pneumonia. Then by chance he met Jai Li through her brother who was one of the poo-bin lads. She came to him when she saw her brother Quan and his friend being loaded into a van; that was the last time she saw him. The boys had been injected and sent home for the night, then the next day they had to report to the laboratory, only to disappear. Several weeks later Jai Li's parents both died of pneumonia. Then one day out of the blue a letter arrived address to her parents; it was from Quan. He gave the letter to the professor to read. It was written proof from one of the company's workers. He also gave him the cutting from the newspaper saying that most of the passengers on a flight from China to America had fallen ill. When checked, this was the fight that Quan was on, so these passengers had been infected. The professor was stunned: here was the proof that he couldn't supply. He rose from his seat and shook both their hands and bowed many times. "Thank you, thank you," he kept repeating.

Here was his evidence unfolding, backed up by actual proof. Chen went on to tell him about the other poo-bin lads that went missing, how an advertisement in the paper caught his eye, so he followed up on it to find many sons were missing. They had been given an injection then sent home for a night so their families could be infected, then they were posted overseas. So many people died of this bad bout of pneumonia that was running rampant, but weeks later it was diagnosed as Covid-19. Once diagnosed, the pharmaceutical laboratory told their workers they had to be vaccinated, so injected them with the virus, which was to silence them from speaking out about the company.

He then went on to talk about Jai Li's death. She had been poisoned by the company (the establishment) by a salesman selling health foods which she consumed. It was meant for both of them, but Chen never ate it. It still brought tears to his eyes as he talked about her, as she was the innocent one! "We will stop here for today. I have to remember all you have told me, so I can formulate it into a manuscript. This is beyond my wildest dreams to have learnt so much from you, actual workers who went through this horrible experience, to have survived and been able to relate this to me. How fortunate I am. How can I thank you enough?" The professor was so happy he stood up and bowed many times to express his gratitude. Chen and Lan Mei thanked him and returned his bows.

The next morning, they were at Mr Yamakawa's office again at 7.45am. He welcomed them with the customary bow and proceeded to tell them he had spent most of the night there, showing them his neat manuscript that was all typed up, very professional indeed! He, like Chen, was eager to carry on where they had left off yesterday. "How did you meet Lan Mei?" he asked. "I was at the shopping centre one day, when Chen recognised me as the office girl from the laboratory, so he came up to me and started talking. We discussed how we hadn't seen any of the other workers and thought that was strange. We agreed to meet in a fortnight's time to see what we had found out. During the time between our next meeting Chen had lost Jai Li, my parents had died of the virus and I had nowhere to live. A few weeks on, Chen asked me to come and live with him at his house. We had discussions on the company and together we dug into its workings, only to discover only three of us had survived. Little did we know the 'establishment' was on to us." "Excuse me, Lan Mei," said Chen, "I have Tan's letter here. Let me give it to the professor to read." He took it out of his backpack and handed it to him.

Upon reading Tan's letter, the professor rubbed his hands together and a huge beam came across his face and the repeated 'thank you, thank you' kept flowing, followed by many more bows. "What happened to your workmate, Tan?" he asked. Chen related the gruesome story, told to him by his wife, that he had been poisoned and had a painful death. He didn't know that it was the health food given to him by his brother that contained the poison.

Lan Mei continued to tell the professor about the salesman trying to sell them health food, and how by this time Chen was on to him. They purchased some and had it tested, only to find it was laced with arsenic. She went on with the story of how the salesman met his fate at their hands and how they disposed of the body. The professor sat forward in his chair, clapping his hands, "More, more," he ordered. There was so much more in between, but the next interesting piece was when the two men from the 'establishment' broke into their house and they ended up killing them too. The professor nearly fell out of his chair, as he had leant that far forward while listening intently to

Lan Mei's story. He jumped up and started clapping louder. "Good girl, good girl," he shouted, then the bowing started all over again. They could tell he was excited; his jubilation was outwardly displayed. "We now have a story, and a true one at that, and all is about to be exposed. How we do it, I haven't worked out yet, as I never visualised we would have living proof, but you two children have 'sealed the deal'. I will forever be indebted to you both as I could not have done this alone. My story was dead in its tracks, but you have brought it back to life."

12

THE VIRUS

CHEN WAS FOLLOWING what was happening with the virus as it had been put aside while they were working with the professor. On the outside world, the virus, now a raging pandemic, was reappearing as a second and third strain. Britain and America along with some European countries were reapplying restrictions, as this new strain was spreading more rapidly than the first. This is what the authorities were frightened of; if it mutated it was more dangerous. Hospital beds in these countries were overflowing and their systems were at tipping point. If you were too sick, you would not be admitted to hospital – you were in the hands of the gods. Even the hospital staff at times had to make decisions on who were put on ventilators; it was like choosing who should live and who should die.

And still Mr Trump was making assumptions amid his election campaign. In his own mind he had won the election, so he spent a lot of time on the golf course. Covid-19 was under control in his country, but only in his thinking, the truth being it was far from contained. Mr Yamakawa was following this with great interest, and he could see there was no end in sight, well, not in the foreseeable future. The virus had turned into a nightmare from which no country was exempt, and neither were any of their citizens. It was a disaster everyone had to live with. For how long, he did not know. What he did know was that China was going to be exposed to the rest of the world. Something this serious was not going to go unanswered.

In the meantime, he had been informed by a colleague in America that a software billionaire had resigned from the company to take an interest in the pharmaceutical industry. He was a shareholder along with two large investment giants, who were institutional shareholders in a well-known drug company. Vaccines were also part of a depopulation agenda promoted to reduce carbon emissions and population growth, through improving healthcare for reproductive services. There were also theories that some vaccines were designed to ensure the reduction of the elderly and people on pensions. Here was exactly the same thing happening with the virus. Was this coincidental?

Anti-virus vaccines were being developed in several countries and were coming on stream faster than first thought; they seemed to be the only answer to halt the virus. Whether they were able to combat the second strain, at this stage no-one knew; like everything else, life had become a lottery with very few winners.

Mr Yamakawa showed Chen and Lan Mei an article in the newspaper that read: 'A global thinktank announced China will take over from the United States as the world's largest economy five years before it was predicted. The contrasting economic recovery after the virus was given as the reason. China can and does crow about its system of government and its effective control of Covid-19, even though it is understood to have begun in the wet markets in Xihan.' "But do we have news for the world," the professor announced. "When we put everything together, China might find itself without many friends!"

Now began the task of where to start with formulating a plan to present to the world a story that was going to take a country down, a powerhouse country, who could upset the world if it so decided. Mr Yamakawa had to weigh up the consequences. Two superpowers against each other; how would this affect the rest of the world? The ante between the two countries was stepping up. Mr Trump's scepticism was disrupting China's plan. His talk of restoring America's greatness was seen by China as an affront to their own dream. But China's role as America's largest banker gave it leverage, as whenever America pressured China to raise the value of its currency, it threatened to sell part of its holding to whoever.

The professor had studied the two great powers. China is the world's largest economy, the largest exporter, the largest consumer of commodities and third largest importer. Cell phones and other household goods made up the largest single category imports from China. Mr Trump's administration has repeatedly complained about China's huge trade surplus with the United States as being unfair. But China argues it should not be punished just because it doesn't buy more US products. He could see dire consequences for both superpowers. How would America handle knowing that the virus was a deliberate ploy to slow down their economy, so China could supersede them as the top superpower? Would this lead to all-out war? In the meantime, he along with Chen and Lan Mei would work together formulating a plan that would stir up the world.

●13

THE PRESENTATION

For weeks they worked on putting together all the facts, the ones they could substantiate with Quan and Tan's letters along with the cuttings Chen had saved. The professor was jubilant with Chen's papers, even if they were kept in a backpack; it wasn't the container that mattered, it was the contents inside. He could see Chen wasn't an educated man, but this didn't stop him from becoming wholly involved in something he believed in. This showed as dedication and, in some instances, that could be more powerful than the most advanced education. He thought Lan Mei was a sweet young girl, but inside there was a tiger and if it was hungry … look out! They were two 'children' the professor would remember forever.

The professor knew he would be classed as both a 'hero' and a 'traitor'. Those that wanted to know the truth would love him, those who chose to ignore the truth would hate him. But controversy was something he sat comfortable with; it had followed him for most of his academic life. This was going to be more controversial and upheaving than anything he had uncovered before, but who was it going to affect most? There was already a growing trade war between China and Australia, all because Australia pushed for an independent enquiry into how the virus started. China's murky role in the spread of the virus had disturbed the whole world. Lax food safety standards have produced periodic scares before, and China is ranked as one of the world's worst food safety offenders.

Would he call a meeting with the heads of state of all countries, or would he publish a book? Either way it was going to be contentious. He could try to get media time, which would soon circle around the world, with the exception of China who would block anything that they classed as propaganda. Perhaps an interview with the media, relying on his position as Nobel Prize winner in Medicine, then drop the bombshell while on air. This would draw media attention; reporters would be on his doorstep, all vying for a piece of the action. That would be his best way of spreading his findings, and hopefully it would draw reporters from far and wide. This is what he wanted: to get the truth out there, not to let the perpetrators get away with their shocking crime. He would discuss it with Chen and Lan Mei as they would have to realise they were part of this. Would they be up for the turbulent times that may lie ahead?

After an in-depth conversation, both Chen and Lan

Mei decided to stand by the professor and back him all the way. They had come this far, so why stop here? Their mission was not yet completed. Now they would wait for the day when the professor went to air. This gave them time to think about themselves. Lan Mei's greatest wish was to make Chen a father, but nothing had happened. Was this due to her disability? She had not discussed this with him for fear of him being upset; it was enough that she was suffering. On the quiet she had asked Mr Yamakawa to find her a doctor who spoke English, so now she had her phone number. One day when Chen was at the professor's office, she called a taxi and went to the doctors. Tests were carried out and her doctor would let her know when the results came back, if there was a reason why she couldn't conceive. Lan Mei felt uncomfortable going behind Chen's back, but she had to put her mind at rest.

Several days later the doctor called and asked her to come to her surgery, so when the opportunity arrived, Lan Mei called a taxi. The doctor asked her if she had had the virus, to which she told her she had. A frown came over the doctor's face; this was not what she wanted to hear. It was now apparent that young females who contacted the virus were now sterile. When she told Lan Mei, she burst into tears. This meant her most cherished wish could never be realised. How was she going to tell Chen? Would he be upset and would he fall out of love with her? Suddenly a flood of hate came over her; this was all because the company she worked for manufactured that terrible virus. Not only did it kill people, it made young women sterile. Was it designed to do this? Was this to slow the world population and stop the weak from breeding? This gave her something else to fight for: she would let it be known to the world … a lost right for young women!

How was she going to tell Chen? She decided to wait until they found a moment of closeness, then she would gently break the news to him. Would he be angry that they could have no children? It was something they had never discussed, and perhaps he didn't want to be a parent. So many scenarios were spinning around in her head. The time had come and Lan Mei couldn't keep it to herself any longer! "Chen, have you ever thought about having children?" He looked at her puzzled. "Why are you asking?" "I have been told by a doctor that I am sterile; does that upset you?" she replied, as tears streamed down her cheeks. Chen looked at her and immediately noticed her tears. "We have each other, and a project we are working on. There wouldn't be time for anyone else in our lives." Lan Mei ran to him and hugged him. "Oh Chen, I'm so sorry, will you still love me?" she asked. He picked her up and carried her through to their bedroom … there lay the answer!

When he found out why she was unable to conceive, he was very angry; in fact, furious. Here was a privilege that had been taken away from young women. Were they on the edge of discovering more fallouts from the virus? Was the world in fact a dangerous place to live? Was this just the start? What could possibly come to light in the future?

At the next meeting with the professor, Lan Mei brought up the new subject that had surfaced. He was bitterly disappointed, and once again it was evidence of China playing with people's lives. "We are living in a virtually unknown world. We are alienated from the past, but what of the future? Let us hope the virus is not here forever; an effective vaccine must bring renewed hope." Such wise words from one in the medical profession, but words were only that, words; they didn't mount to much in these unsettled times. Vaccines were never going to help the young women who wanted to be mothers, their lives ruined, never to be righted; it was a privilege lost forever!

A date had been set for the news broadcast when the professor was going to speak about his Nobel Prize in Medicine. It would be during this talk he would drop the bombshell. He knew he could be closed down on air, but if he could get the accusation on China out, it would bring the hungry reporters baying for blood to his workplace. There, he along with Chen and Lan Mei would present all the evidence needed to create a storm. The media would love this; it would be a race to see what paper got the information out first and which one would be prepared to pay the right price for the whole story. The professor wanted to secure a future for Chen and Lan Mei so of course the highest bidder would secure the rights. He wanted 'his children' to live a comfortable life, for all the sadness they had endured throughout their short lives, as it was a miracle they had survived at all. And what a story they had lived to tell! They had a week to discuss how they were going to formulate the handling of the media.

Finally, the big day arrived. Chen and Lan Mei accompanied the professor to the studio, as he had asked them to come with him. They were shown into a small office until it was time for the professor to go into the recording studio, where he was to be interviewed. He brought along his briefcase with all his notes, not that he needed them, as he had everything in his head. He would go along with the questions, but the minute he got a lead he would unleash his attack on China, knowing it was a risk, as he could be cut off the airwaves in a flash. But it was a risk he was prepared to take, as he wanted to ignite a flame that would spread like wildfire! "Professor, will you please come through, you will be on air in five minutes," instructed the announcer. He took Chen and Lan Mei through to a small room off the studio where they could see and hear the interview. They sat and held hands; this was the moment of truth, the moment they had worked so hard to bring out in the open, in other words, to expose the perpetrator!

The interviewer asked many questions which the professor answered politely, then his moment came. "Professor, what are you currently working on? Our listeners would like to know what is coming next." This was his time to seize the moment. "I have been working alongside two young colleagues on a subject dear to all our hearts, perhaps some more than others. By some, I mean families who have lost loved ones to the virus. Each day thousands of people are dying. Why? we ask ourselves; where did the virus start and how? I have living proof this is a manufactured virus that was released by China. The laboratory it was manufactured in was the workplace of my two colleagues, the only two known survivors outside of the 'establishment'. This was done for political gain ..." "I'm sorry, Professor, we have to end it there. Thank you for coming in today to speak with us." There the broadcast ended. Had he said enough to stir the public's interest, but more importantly had he caught the media's attention? An overwhelming feeling of triumph flooded through Chen and Lan Mei: the professor had done it! They were sure this would open a hornet's nest, circulating stinging accusations throughout the world. But would there be repercussions? This they had accepted, as now not only were they murderers and arsonists but they had become traitors to their country of origin, and their safety could be in jeopardy. Chen shook the professor's hand, acknowledging that he was happy with the interview. A reporter cut in: "Excuse me, Professor, what were you saying? You actually have proof of your fairly out-there accusations, and politically motivated, what strong words. There will be some unhappy people." The professor qualified his remarks: "Yes, but there will also be some questions answered as to how and why. People's lives are not to be played with for political gain, and this is what is happening around the world right now. But it has gone too far, it has spiralled out of control. One country wants to rule the world, so how do they do it – they weaken the economy of the rest of the world, knowing they have control in their hands. It all comes down to being the 'top superpower' at the expense of innocent people who are dying like flies. This is not justice; this is murder!"

As they were leaving the building there were several reporters waiting in the carpark … word was out! "Tell us more, Professor. How do you know it was a manufactured virus and not a natural one?" a reporter asked. "I will hold a press conference at my office tomorrow morning at 10.30, so if you want answers, be there." This was a pretty blunt reply, but hopefully it would have the desired effect. This let the other reporters know where to be if they wanted answers. While driving home, the chatter was full of excitement. What was going to greet them in the morning? Would there only be a few reporters or would his office be swarming with them? "Come to my office and we will watch the local news. Perhaps there may be something on my interview. I will order in some food; we will eat here," he told Chen and Lan Mei. They sat round talking until the food arrived, then they settled in to eat. Mr Yamakawa put the television on, as the news was about to start. It was all about the virus and how many people were dying as a result of it and how the second strain was rampant in the United Kingdom, spreading faster than the first, and there seemed to be no answers as to how to stop it. Other countries were introducing more stringent measures to ensure this new strain didn't enter their borders. In fact, overseas flights were being diverted away from the worst-hit countries. Once again, the world was in a spin! Then it all happened.

'Today Mr Yamakawa, the Nobel Prize winner in

Medicine, was interviewed in a local studio and he dropped a bombshell. The listeners flooded the switchboard with calls, reporters from around the globe were trying to make contact, to get information first hand from the studio that did the interview. Due to the pandemic, no overseas reporters could fly into Tokyo, but they wanted information as to where contact could be made with the professor. Everyone who heard the interview wants to know the truth about the virus, and this has sparked a nationwide outburst. The professor is giving an interview at his office in the morning. We will be there and will bring an update to our news tomorrow night. "We have done it, Professor, we have done it," yelled a delighted Chen.

The next morning as Chen and Lan Mei neared Mr Yamakawa's office, the streets ahead were swallowed up with traffic. They could not believe their eyes; were they all here to listen to the professor? People were lined up in the streets in front of his office. The media were there with their cameras and tripods, all vying to get a scoop for their newspapers. Chen and Lan Mei excused themselves as they moved through the people to get to the office. "Professor, have you seen the crowds outside? How are you going to handle them?" Chen asked. "Don't worry, children, I have handled crowds before, and once I start, they will listen. All they want to know is the truth. I want you both to stand alongside me, as there will probably be questions asked of you. We will only tell them so much. If I cut in when you are being questioned, it is because we don't want too much disclosed at this point in time.

Remember we are selling our story to the highest bidder, and this is for your future. You must be compensated for the heartbreak you have suffered on this journey. We are here to uncover a conspiracy, to make it public so everyone knows. It will not be easy for us, but this is our choice, and we have the ammunition needed to expose a country that has put power before the people."

"Come out, Professor and tell us the truth; we need to know," people were chanting from the street. It was now time for the trio to show their faces in public. Mr Yamakawa came out first, dressed in his suit and tie, looking every bit the professional man that he was. Chen and Lan Mei followed, greeted with cheers and applause from the crowds. Mr Yamakawa bowed to his audience and began. "Welcome everyone. My colleagues and I have all the evidence needed to let the world know how, why and where the virus began. China wants us to believe the virus was a natural cause, associated with animals then passed on to humans, but this is far from the truth. The virus was manufactured in a laboratory situated next to the named wet market. My colleagues both worked for the laboratory and since it closed down, they were lucky enough to have survived several attempts on their life, by the 'establishment'. We have proof of how the virus spread so quickly to so many countries and why so many of the laboratory workers died. Their deaths were planned by the 'establishment' to silence them so they were not available to comment on what happened at their workplace." This caused an uproar from the crowd. "How did they silence the workers?" people wanted to know.

"They were given an injection, which they were told was a flu shot, but in reality, it was the virus they were injected with." "No, no, that can't be true?" came the response from the crowd. "Yes, that is the truth, horrible as it may be, but I swear upon my Nobel Prize. The workers were used as guinea pigs. Young men were injected with the virus then put on planes and sent to different countries. They didn't know they were carriers of the virus; they like their fellow workers were told it was a flu injection. They were given a one-way ticket as the 'establishment' knew they were never going to survive to need a return ticket. These young men were murdered by their superiors! This is what our world has come to: lives don't matter; power is what rules! ... My colleague Lan Mei would like to add to this as she has a grievance of her own," finished the professor.

"Like many young women here," Lan Mei began, "I wanted to become a mother, but this privilege has been taken from me. I contracted the virus as a healthy young person, I survived but became a cripple only to learn that I am now sterile; this is how the virus has left me. If you are of child-bearing age and have been unlucky and caught the virus, you will find you are now sterile. We, as future mothers, have been penalised: we can bear no children. Is this also what it was designed for, to stop the weak from producing and to control the population, I ask myself?" There was an uproar from the crowd: who was this young lady? Suddenly a hostility towards China surfaced and people were angry. They had no idea of the consequences of the virus, and of the deaths that had occurred, simply because what happened in China was meant to stay in China. The crowd were soon silenced by the professor: "Let us remain calm. These are the results of one country wanting to take over the world, of how greed and power combined can overrule the value of human lives. Healthy people become guinea pigs, old people are of no use, weak people have lost the right to breed, so what are we left with?" Applause rang out loud and clear from the crowd. "This is not the end; more allegations will be forthcoming, as will denials, but my colleagues and I speak the truth, as we have nothing to hide. This is all, so please go home and reflect on what you have heard from us today … goodbye!"

After the streets emptied, a few stragglers stayed behind to haggle with the professor. They were supporters of the Chinese Government. "Stop preaching propaganda. You will pay for this," they yelled.

The evening news was full of the interview with the professor and his colleagues. Media from all around the world were reporting on the 'China conspiracy'. Countries were outraged to learn what had transpired, as up until now it was believed to be a natural virus started in China, which was not unusual as previous virus outbreaks began there, due to its poor food standards. America was furious, and Mr Trump let everyone know that he had predicted this in the early stages of the virus, but his Twitter account was ridiculed by the world, so his stupidity had disguised the truth. Next came the backlash from China. This was all propaganda, none of it was true, who were these people making these false accusations?

The professor had many offers for the full story and the evidence, but it was on sale to the highest bidder. This was about the future of his 'children', as the path ahead was going to be far from plain sailing. He wasn't worried about himself; his life was all but over. His mission was nearly completed and all he wanted was to bring down the perpetrators, to expose China for what they did to the world. So many unnecessary deaths, so much financial loss, all for the reward to become the one and only superpower. Now it was up to the rest of the world to band together and punish China for its misgivings.

14

WHAT CAME NEXT!

Mr Yamakawa had noted Lan Mei's love of bonsai trees, so he approached a local grower to secure a position in his nursery for her, so she could learn how to grow and shape them. As he was an influential man in his home town, his request was granted. She was overwhelmed with joy as these little trees had become her second love after Chen. She had loved them from her first glance; they intrigued her, bringing a warm feeling to her heart. She didn't know why, as she never knew they existed before coming to Japan. Was this telling her she had found her place of peace? Chen was now a constant companion of the professor, helping him with his virus research, and what the impact would be on China, if all the countries boycotted them.

Being realistic, the professor knew it would take years to completely diversify away from China, but the current situation was unacceptable; Covid had made that clear. A need for a new trading system was overdue, and it would be better than continuing to base health welfare for the rest of the world on the decisions of the Chinese Communist Party. More viruses were sure to emerge from China, as had been proven in the past. Despite its vast size, China was land poor. Therefore, it depends on America, as it is the top provider of food imports to that country, mainly meat, seafood, dairy products and soy beans. If the ties were cut, where would America sell its produce? So much depends on imports and exports between these two superpowers. Did the growth of Chinese investment in many foreign countries allow them to farm land, so as to supply China with the food needed in the future? Was this planned to secure their own food chain? This was what the professor and Chen were researching.

Several weeks had passed since the professor's live on-air interview, and many offers had come in for his full story. The top bid was from an American talkshow, who had an office-studio in Tokyo. Because of the borders being closed, they could not fly the three of them to America, so offered for them to stay in a hotel in Tokyo and do a live broadcast from their studio there. The offer far exceeded what the professor had in mind, and after talking it over with Chen and Lan Mei, they decided to accept the deal put before them. "This money is for you both, my wish is that it secures you a future, so you can have a good life," the professor told them. Chen argued that the professor take some of the money, but he would not hear of 'such nonsense'. "I have money of my own, and

I don't need any more as I have no family. You are my children."

A week later they flew into Tokyo and were met at the airport by an American news reporter, and after introductions they were taken to the hotel, which was in the vicinity of the Tokyo Tower. It looked spectacular as it stretched above many high-rise buildings, and the silhouette of the brightly coloured Tower reminded Lan Mei of the beautiful Oriental Pearl Tower in Shanghai. Not that the memories from that place were very pleasant. Their accommodation was a lovely boutique hotel with exquisite furnishings and hostesses dressed in traditional kimonos. They were made very welcome by many bows, which by now they were accustomed to. Their American host left them to have two days to themselves for sightseeing, then he would pick them up for the all-important live talk. Lan Mei was most impressed with their studio suite, with all the little niceties. Mr Yamakawa was in a suite next door.

The next two days passed so quickly, and Lan Mei had a great time buying new clothes, a privilege she had never had before. Chen wanted her to look nice for the interview, as they were going to be seen all over America and possibly further afield. She was grateful for the fortune that had come their way, but it was not without its challenges. The morning had arrived, they were in the foyer waiting to be picked up, when a man rushed into the hotel brandishing a gun, which he aimed at the professor. There was a loud bang and the professor fell to the floor. Everyone was stunned. Chen rushed to his aid as did the hotel staff. The professor struggled to sit up but then fell backwards. He grabbed Chen's arm. "You have to go ahead with the live talkshow. It is your time now," then he fell unconscious. Lan Mei watched as it all unfolded. She saw the gunman run up the hallway so she hurried towards him as best she could, then he closed a door, marked 'Storeroom'. A cleaner's trolley was parked in the hallway outside the door so she pushed it against the door and called for help. Several staff members appeared and when she indicated that the gunman was in the storeroom, one produced a master key and locked the door. The police were called, but then a shot was fired; he taken his own life was the general assumption. "Oh no!" someone screamed, when she recognised the trolley. It belonged to her friend who was restocking it to bring back to a suite. Panic among the staff began. Was she behind the locked door with the gunman, and who was dead, the gunman or the cleaner?

The manager appeared at that moment and when he realised the seriousness of the situation, he called on his speaker phone and asked all cleaning staff to come immediately to the storeroom. All but one appeared, so they knew then she must have been in the storeroom. As they were huddled together, a trickle of blood seeped from under the door, sending chills down their spines. The manager made the decision not to unlock the door until the police arrived in case the gunman was still alive. Lan Mei left and went to the foyer only to see the professor being carried out to a waiting ambulance. There, still huddled on the floor was Chen, in disbelief at what had just happened. His mentor had been shot … but why? Lan Mei helped him up and took him in her arms. They cried together.

The American news reporter arrived in the midst of it all and was shocked when he learned what had happened. Chen and Lan Mei were still shedding tears, their dear friend was now on his way to hospital, and they didn't know how badly hurt he was. The reporter told them the talkshow began in an hour and it would have to go on. "I'm sorry, but we can't cancel, our time slot has been advertised, so many people are desperately waiting on this live interview. We have been inundated with calls, and they all want to know the truth on the virus. Let me get you to the studio so you can relax until you go on air." They went along with what was expected of them, as they had not fully recovered from what had just taken place. At the studio they sat together and held hands; the professor was foremost on their minds. Lan Mei worried about the cleaning girl? This all had to be forgotten at the moment, as it was only a matter of minutes before they would be on the talkshow, and this was the professor's last request.

Three … two … one … on air live. "First, we must apologise for the absence of the professor. He was caught up in a random shooting at his hotel and is in hospital. We don't know how severe his injuries are, but we do have his two colleagues, Chen and Lan Mei, with us today to answer our questions. First we would like to know how you befriended the professor." Chen explained about the pamphlet that was circulating underground. Here was a man brave enough to accuse China of a grave injustice.

These were his exact thoughts, and he had the facts. All he knew was he was a Nobel Prize winner in Medicine, so they went to the library and read about him. Then found a website under one of his articles, so that was how the connection happened. "Tell me about the laboratory. What made you suspicious of its activities?" Chen told the whole story from start to finish, starting with the missing poo-bin lads and their grieving parents who went to their graves not knowing what happened to their sons. Then how the virus was spread to each country. "I believe your company tried several times to dispense with you both, but you fought for your lives. Please tell us what happened?" Chen carried on explaining all that was asked of him. "Now Lan Mei, you mentioned what disabilities the virus left you with. Please tell us about them." She told her story, and tears streamed down her face as she related how her most wanted wish, to make Chen a father, had been taken from her. "I am not the only one to suffer; all female virus victims of childbirth age will end up sterile. I am worried what other defects will arise from the virus."

"One last question for you both: how did you feel about leaving your home country of China?" Chen said he was speaking on behalf of them both. They didn't recognise China as their country of origin any more, as it had brought shame and loss to so many people. Their new homeland was now Japan, and this is where they felt happy. "We are very sorry about the professor, please give him our best wishes. We will finish this show so you can be with him. We would love to have you back again one day along with the professor. Thank you very much for being brave enough to come forward with the truth. It is ordinary people like yourselves who are our eyes and ears on the world. Goodbye for now."

They were driven back to their hotel where they couldn't wait to get to reception and find out what happened after they left. The front desk lady told them they had lost an employee and the police ended up shooting the gunman as he had threatened to shoot his way out. "How can we get in touch with the professor?" Lan Mei asked. She was given the hospital phone number, which she rung straight away, only to be told he was in the operating theatre, that the bullet had lodged in his spine. This was of grave concern. If he lived, what injuries would this leave him with?

Chen and Lan Mei were told they could stay at the hotel as long as it took for the professor to recover. They sat by his bedside every day, willing him to wake up and speak to them. It took several days before an announcement was made public; he was paralysed from the waist down and would live the rest of his life in a wheelchair. When his 'children' heard this news, they cried together. Such a great man reduced to a life in a wheelchair, how would he look after himself? This was when Lan Mei made a promise to herself: she would become his caregiver. He had given them a new life in a new country, now it was their time to repay him for his kindness. She was sure Chen would feel the same.

Meanwhile the feedback from the live talkshow was that it was a roaring success. It had aired throughout America and now many other countries were trying to secure the rights. It was worldwide news because the virus was a pandemic and people wanted to know the how, when and why. Immediate action was needed as thousands of people were dying. The American people loved Chen and Lan Mei and demanded that they come back, and the studio was inundated with requests for them to return. Would they accept donations? A lot of money had been sent to the studio to set up a trust for them. But they decided they wouldn't accept the money for themselves, but if the donors agreed, perhaps the money could go to helping families in China, who were struggling to survive without their loved ones. Chen would do this through Tan's widow, definitely not through the government, as their sentiment was not with the people. He remembered her words when he asked if she could manage without Tan. 'It will be hard, but I am one of many who will struggle to survive.' He felt deep compassion for those whose family members were taken from them, as he had experienced that pain. Lan Mei was his salvation; she was a brave young lady who bore scars from the virus but accepted her disabilities and got on with life. They were a strength to one another.

Today when they went to visit the professor, he was up and dressed and seated in his wheelchair. The nurses had showered and got him ready for his visitors. "Well, 'children', in a few days we will be ready to go home. I will have to go into care as I can't do for myself. Not the life I expected to be living in my latter years, but I don't have a choice." Lan Mei reached for his hand. "No, Professor you will not be going into care. Chen and I will be your caregivers; we will come and live with you, if this is agreeable to you." Tears filled the professor's eyes, as he never expected this. He did not protest but accepted graciously. To have the company of two young people on his estate was a comforting thought. Information from the talkshow was now circulating the world, and the professor and his colleagues were being hailed as heroes. Reporters waited eagerly outside the hospital trying to get a glimpse of them, but Chen and Lan Mei were not limelight people so shied away when possible.

15

REVISITING CHINA

THE FLIGHT from Tokyo landed at Nagoya airport carrying the professor and his colleagues. Chen accompanied him as he was lifted off the plane in his wheelchair, while Lan Mei attended to the paperwork. She had picked up on the Japanese language very quickly so was able to communicate with the authorities. A special access van was waiting for them, to take the professor to his home. Chen and Lan Mei had no idea where he lived as they only knew of his flat, where they lived, and his office. The van passed through the city and into a suburban area where there were large homes on larger blocks of land. The driver slowed down and drove into a driveway, "We are home, 'children,'" announced the professor. Chen and Lan Mei were caught off guard. Surely he didn't live here on his own in this big house? No wonder he wouldn't take any of the money for the sale of their story, he must have plenty in order to live here, they both thought. As they pulled up outside the house Lan Mei noticed a huge glasshouse that was housing bonsai trees. "You didn't tell me you grew bonsai, Professor," she said. "This was to be a surprise, as one day this will all belong to you and Chen. I wanted you to be taught properly how to grow them, as you now know there are secrets in the growing." Lan Mei took his hand, "You are a dear man. Yes, I have learned the secrets of bonsai growing, and you know, they are my favourite plants." "Come 'children', we will go inside." Chen helped the professor get his chair over the little step as they entered the house. The step, he thought, would be his first renovation to make the house wheelchair friendly. But how on earth was he going to manage the upstairs rooms? The inside was furnished with expensive ornaments, but it lacked a woman's touch, and a little colour wouldn't go astray, thought Lan Mei. The professor showed her where everything was in the kitchen and asked if she would make them a pot of tea.

It was all settled; Chen and Lan Mei would live in the upstairs of the house and the professor would live on the ground floor. A home help would come in every morning and shower and dress him, then it was up to both of them to care for him. He decided to sell his office block and rent out the flat, as he would work from home. Chen's first job was to make sure the house was totally wheelchair friendly, so the professor could move around safely by himself, as there would be times when he would want to do his own thing.

The American media were still trying to get a second

live talkshow, as they were being pressured by the public to bring Chen and Lan Mei back on air. The trust money had built up to a substantial figure, so now it was up to Chen to get the money to Tan's widow in China, who would then distribute it to those in need. But how? Would it be safe for him to take the ferry back to China without being recognised? If the authorities of that country got whiff of him being there, he would just disappear like so many others who spoke out about the virus or the government. It would be a huge risk; was he prepared to take it? How would Lan Mei and the professor feel about it?

Tonight was the night to break the news to Lan Mei and the professor. Chen had thought it over and over, but the desire to help those people that the 'establishment' had robbed of a breadwinner and who were struggling to survive overwhelmed all other feelings. This he had to do! After they finished dinner Chen asked them to remain at the table as he had an announcement to make. "Please hear me out. I am going back to China with the money from the live talkshow trust, to give to Tan's widow who will then give it to people in need. It is in my heart that I do this; I must help those that our company disadvantaged, as the suffering for them has been horrendous. I have to put it right." Lan Mei was in shock, but she knew he was suffering in his heart, for the misgivings of their company. She leaned over and kissed him. The professor sat in silence. What would he do without one of his children? But he understood Chen's concern for his people, as he was a caring soul, and he knew his heart was telling him it was his duty to take this risk. "I will arrange with Toshi and her people to get you a safe passage into China; they will look after you. I will deposit the money into her bank account and she will give it to you once you have reached your destination. This way, if you are searched you will have nothing to hide. You will have to pay her from the money, but I'm sure the donors will understand.

Several days passed and the professor had spoken with Toshi and all was arranged. Chen decided to lighten his hair colour and his eyebrows. He would wear a hat pulled down on his head and a face mask. His long trousers would cover his shoes which had thicker heels, thus making him look taller. He borrowed them from the professor, who always wanted people to think he was taller than he actually was. Marcel would meet him when he got off the train in Osaka and make sure he caught the ferry to Shanghai, where he would be met by Toshi. She would drive him to Xihun where she would drop him off for two days to do his business, then she would drive him back to Shanghai. If it all went to plan Chen would be home in ten days. Lan Mei was happy with these arrangements, and she felt nothing could go wrong. She would look after the professor while Chen was away. She would take him out with her to the glasshouse where he could help her with the bonsai, as they both shared the same love for these special miniature trees.

Tonight was their last night together, then the separation – she would miss his arms not surrounding her, so an early night was on the cards! Lan Mei wanted to make love, to have happy memories while Chen was away. He was a willing participant so off to bed they went. There was mayhem in the bedroom, a tornado tore the bedclothes off the bed, leaving two naked bodies exposed to the elements. Not that either of them noticed, as they were so entangled in each other, an earthquake couldn't have disturbed them. Lan Mei enjoyed making love to Chen. She had lost her inhibitions so there was no holding back; she became the huntress hungry for her prey. Several hours later, two exhausted bodies pulled up the tangled bedclothes and dropped off to sleep.

●16

THE JOURNEY

As the train pulled to a stop at Osaka station, Chen looked out the window and could see Marcel standing on the platform. As he alighted from the train, he waved to him so they walked towards each other and shook hands. "You look different, Chen. I hardly recognised you," said Marcel. "Yes, I am wearing the professor's shoes with built-up heels, and I've changed the colour of my hair and eyebrows. I can't afford to be recognised or I will never make it back to Japan. Do you know if they still have a reward out for Lan Mei and me?" He couldn't enlighten Chen on this, but he said Toshi would know as she was their Chinese informer. As they drove to the ferry terminal, Marcel told Chen, "I have booked your cabin, but to be on the safe side hang low, in case the police are still looking for you." Chen asked Marcel if he had seen their live talkshow. He hadn't, but he had heard people talking about it, and he hadn't realised that they were the whistle-blowers on China. "You be very careful, Chen. Should you be caught, the Chinese authorities will show you no mercy. Toshi will look after you, but she is very wary of the authorities, as they can be brutal. She has witnessed this with her own eyes, that is why she formed her own company, to help ship people out of China to safety, through her underground movement. We are at the terminal, so I will give you your tickets. Be careful my friend, I will see you on your return journey."

The ferry crossing to China went without incident, as Chen elected to spend most of his time in his cabin. He noticed when he boarded that there was still police presence on the ferry as well as at the terminal. The familiar blast of the horn let him know it was time to pack his bags and make his way to the deck. As he was making his way down the gangway he was stopped by the police and asked how long he was spending in China. Chen thought for a minute. He didn't want them watching out for his return, so he said twelve days, but by then he would be back in Japan, all going to plan. He was told to carry on. It took him an hour to find Toshi at the busy terminal, as she didn't recognise him until he mentioned the password, 'Mr X'. "Chen, you look so different, you are taller than I remember." Chen burst into laughter as he told her about wearing Mr Yamakawa's shoes. "Come, we will drive all night and day until we reach Xihun, as I am well rested. The professor told me all about your talkshow and blowing China right out in the open. How brave! You will have to be extremely careful while back here. The broadcast has been banned here in

China and has been reported as propaganda by the authorities." Chen asked if there was still a reward out for Lan Mei and himself. "Yes, but it is not at the forefront, as they know you have left the country. In fact, I heard they had sent an assassin to Japan to take out the professor as they know he is popular there; is he okay?" When Chen told her he was now confined to a wheelchair, she was sad to hear this. This now confirmed to Chen who was behind the shooting.

As they neared Xihun, Toshi pulled over to the side of the road and switched her number plates. "Just a precautionary procedure, then no-one will know where I am." Chen remembered her doing the exact same thing when she drove them last time. "I have the money in my briefcase. You take it and do what you have to do, and I will pick you up in two days' time at the crossroads on the southern end of town, say, Tuesday at 8.30am. We will then drive straight through to Shanghai then on to the ferry terminal. We won't hang around; best to get you out of China as soon as possible." Now he had to find where Tan's wife lived. He knew the area but had no idea of the street name, but, luckily, he knew her surname. Toshi dropped him off in the vicinity, and now it was up to him. "Be careful, Chen, keep your hat pulled down, and good luck my friend," then she drove off.

Chen felt abandoned; this didn't seem like his country any more, and he hated that it had punished the rest of the world just to gain power. He would do his deed and hoped he never had to come back. Perhaps the professor could arrange through Toshi to deliver the next lot of trust money. It was just that he had to explain to Tan's widow about the money and how he wanted it distributed.

Chen walked all afternoon trying to find Mrs Jiang, Tan's widow, but no-one seemed to know of her. He was obviously in the wrong area. But he would not be beaten; he was on a mission and he would see it through. By dusk he finally had a lead, so made his way to the address given to him. He knocked on the door and it was opened by a young boy. "Is Mrs Jiang home?" he asked. "Mother, someone to see you," the child yelled. When she came to the door, yes, he recognised her. She looked at him, puzzled. "What do you want?" she asked. Of course, she didn't remember him as she had only met him once. Chen explained who he was and she invited him in. He told her his story to which she listened in total disbelief: "I have a large amount of money in my briefcase; it is from a trust that was formed in Japan. I want you to share it with all the laboratory workers who have lost the family breadwinner." She burst into tears, as their life had been a struggle with no help forthcoming from the government for families. In fact no-one had receive help of any kind. One of the children asked why she was crying. "We have just been given some money from this kind man from Japan," she explained to him. Her three children had gone without, as they could barely afford to eat.

"Oh Chen, this is like a miracle, how can we thank you? You are like a god who has arrived in the hour of need. So many families will benefit from this, as many are on the edge of starvation. When he told her how much money was in the briefcase, it brought on more tears. She jumped up and hugged him. "I will hide the money in a pillowcase then sew it up, in case we are ever searched." "Please keep this quiet and feed it to the people discreetly; don't divulge where it came from," requested Chen. The widow asked if she could share the secret with her best friend in case anything went amiss. She gave Chen her name in case he needed to contact her. "Where are you staying?" she asked. He told her he had nothing arranged. "My friend lives on her own. Stay with her and you can explain about the money; it will be safe for you there." She rang and arranged for Chen to go to her house. He was secretly pleased that he didn't have to look for accommodation, as this saved him the worry of being recognised, although he knew no-one in this neighbourhood.

The next day Chen went back to visit Tan's widow. The children had gone off to school, so he was able to talk more freely about the money and to enquire if any more workers were known to have survived, but alas, it was not good news. She showed Chen where she had hidden the money in the pillowcase until she was able to start distributing it. He asked if she thought it would be safe for him to go to his old workplace to see what had been done, if anything, but she advised him not to. She said she hadn't been near, as it held sad memories. "Did you know Tan's brother went missing? No-one knows what happened to him, and his body has not been found." Of course Chen knew, as Tan's brother was the man they made eat the poisoned health food, then got rid of his body over a cliff. But this was his and Lan Mei's secret, and no-one must ever know. These things were best left unspoken.

Only one more night, then he was being picked-up by Toshi. He liked the lady he was staying with; her name was Lanying. She seemed a sensible person and she told him that Tan's wife took a long time to get over his death; it was only the children that kept her sane. They decided to go and visit her for the last time before Chen left. When they arrived, the door was wide open and the house had been ransacked. "What the hell is going on here?" asked an alarmed Chen. A neighbour came over and told them the authorities had packed the family into a van and taken them away. Apparently one of the children had gone to school and told a teacher that a man from Japan had brought heaps of money to their house. Chen had to turn away, the tears streamed down his face. Surely, they weren't going to hurt the family? Then he remembered the pillowcase and where it was hidden, so he entered the house and, yes, it was still there, so he picked it up and said to Lanying, "Let's get out of here quick." They left immediately. Chen was heartbroken; had he been the cause for this family to be taken away? What would happen to them? He never thought for a moment that the children would mention the money, but if they were excited, they had to tell someone, and unfortunately it was their teacher, who took it further! Now the trust money was in Lanying's hands, and she assured Chen that she knew who her friend wanted to help, so she would carry on with the original arrangements. She knew it had to be distributed to the surviving families that had worked at the laboratory. They were the ones suffering most, as their loved ones had been injected with the deadly virus. "Lanying, please make sure when the money is distributed there are no children privy to what is happening, as this has sent out a warning." She totally agreed.

That night in bed Chen sobbed uncontrollably. What had happened to Tan's family? Could he ever forgive himself if they had suffered, and how would he ever find out? This, he knew, was what happened in China: if one disobeyed the rules punishment was inevitable and this could be brutal at times. But a family ... surely they would be spared, but in his own mind, he knew what the authorities were capable of and forgiveness wasn't on their agenda. Then he began to wonder if they would torture Tan's widow, to make her tell who delivered the money, and if this was so, he was right in the firing line. The authorities would be furious if they knew the whistle-blower was back in the country. The police would be out in force. Perhaps Toshi could fill him in tomorrow morning, but first he had to get through the night.

When morning eventually arrived, Chen was a nervous wreck. Lanying had made him breakfast, but he had to refuse, as the very thought of food made him feel sick. "You must eat, Chen, as you have a big day in front of you," she reminded him. He couldn't even force himself; all his feelings were for the family. What had happened to them? "Lanying, please give me your phone number so I can call you, I must know the family are safe. It would be dangerous if I left my number with you. I will ring you tonight while we are driving to Shanghai. Try to find out what you can today; it is driving me insane." On this note they had to say their goodbyes as it was time for Chen to be on his way if he was going to be on time to meet up with Toshi.

He had just turned the corner at the end of the street when he saw the police cordoning off the street where Tan's widow lived. There were guards everywhere, stopping all the cars, making the people get out, then searching them. Chen felt terrified. He was carrying his bag and the briefcase, which he thought was a dead giveaway. There was a hedge surrounding the next property, so he quickly moved closer and stuffed his briefcase into the hedge, hoping it would just disappear. He didn't stop to check but picked up his pace and carried on. How he wished he was in Toshi's car speeding away from all of this! The authorities must have got information from Tan's widow and now the roadblocks were being put in place. He was almost running to make it to their meeting place. Thank goodness they had arranged an early pick-up before the whole area was blocked off. True to form, Toshi pulled up just as Chen arrived, so he quickly jumped into her car and told her to 'boot it'. "Chen, I have just heard the news: a family has been apprehended, they were visited by a man from Japan who left a case full of money. Apparently, the children spoke about it at school, so the police are searching the property at this very moment for the money. What on earth happened, and where is my briefcase?" He quickly explained what had taken place, amid his tears. "I'm devastated. What will happen to the family, Toshi?" She knew in her own mind, but elected not to tell Chen, as it would destroy him. "Let us get out of here, as they will looking for you," she told him. They drove in silence, and what was there to say anyway? Toshi could see Chen was heartbroken over Tan's family. As they left the outskirts she pulled over and did another number-plate switch.

Just on dusk, Chen decided to make his phone call to Lanying to see if she had found out about the family. It was driving him mad; he had to know. "Hi, Lanying, what news do you have for me?" he asked. There was a hesitation on the end of the phone; how was she going to tell him? There was only one thing to do and that was to tell the truth. "This afternoon they bulldozed the house down, and no-one knows what has happened to the children, but my friend has been jailed. She has been named as an informer." "Oh my God, what have I done? I wanted them to have a better life, but all I have brought is more grief. What can I do?" he asked. "Sad as it may be, Chen, we can do nothing, but think of all the other families the money will help; it has not all been in vain. Sometimes people suffer to make good for others, and this is what has happened here! When you do your next live talkshow, let the world know what has happened today along with the misery our people are suffering, and how many families the trust money has helped. Let them know how grateful we are, Chen, as our own government doesn't care about its people. Thank you, my friend." There the conversation ended.

Chen related the call from Lanying to Toshi. "Don't beat yourself up my friend. Terrible things are happening all over the word today, sacrifices are being made, people are dying, good deeds are few and far between, but life just goes on, and we must make the best of each day. You are doing a good deed by caring for the professor. Just think, he would have had to go into a home, but now he can enjoy his latter years in his home environment being looked after by two caring friends. You have not failed. This was just an unfortunate incident; it was beyond your control. Let it go and focus on what a difference you can make to more lives," Toshi told him. Chen went very quiet. He needed to put the past two days behind him and move on; he knew in himself he was a good soul. As much as he would like, he couldn't solve the problems of the world.

They drove all night and arrived in Shanghai at 7.30am, in the midst of the early-morning peak-hour traffic. Toshi drove through the city and headed straight to the ferry terminal, which took another hour, as they weaved their way through the traffic. The ferry wasn't due to leave for another two hours, so they went to Toshi's office in the terminal. There weren't many passengers waiting for the ferry, now that the border restrictions were in force. Not like the last time when all residents from China and Japan were returning to their respective countries, because of the virus. Toshi told Chen to rest, and she would purchase his ferry ticket, for fear that he might be recognised. While doing this she noticed a line-up of police officers waiting at the ticket office asking to see people's passports. Most knew Toshi, so she let them know she was purchasing a ticket for her cousin who was returning to Japan. "Not many people travelling at the moment, so why are there so many police?" she enquired. The answer came back from several of the officers, "Haven't you heard the news? Apparently the 'whistle-blower' has come back into the country. He was in the Xihun province, but they have cordoned the town off, so tomorrow there will be double the guards here, as he is thought to be heading back to Japan, if he is not caught in the meantime." Toshi heaved a sigh of relief. Thank goodness Chen was leaving tonight, before the heavy artillery arrived tomorrow. She wondered if she should tell him, then decided against it, as he would probably appear more nervous if approached. It would be better if he was relaxed, well, as relaxed as he could be, amid his current worries, as he was not the same Chen that had arrived four days ago. Tan's family saga had taken a toll on him, and he was suffering inwardly.

"Time to board the ferry, Chen. Here is your ticket. I will accompany you to the gangway. If anyone should approach, tell them you are 'Toshi's cousin'. That's what I told them at the ticket office. If I stand with you until the last horn sounds, they will see us together. Then you can make a dash to board. Make yourself scarce while sailing; stay in your cabin." They stood and talked until the last blast sounded. She put her arms around him and whispered, "Take care my friend, love to Lan Mei and the professor. Go now!" As Chen made his way to board, he heard her calling, "Goodbye dear cousin," so he turned and waved. This was his final farewell to China; he never wanted to set foot on Chinese soil ever again. All he wanted was to get home to Lan Mei and the professor. They had made a pact that he wouldn't contact them while in China, so if things did go wrong, they couldn't trace them.

Once on board, Chen went straight to his cabin, took off his shoes and lay on the bed, as he was mentally exhausted. He would only leave his cabin to get food when he was hungry, as he had noticed a heavy police presence on board. It added to his mental turmoil. His brain had never stop working overtime since all started going wrong, and now he had time to rethink the past few days. China hadn't changed, people were still struggling, although if one listened to the news coming out of Beijing, it painted a rosy picture, which was absolute rubbish! Beijing only printed what it wanted the world to believe, and truth never came into the equation. What other country would treat a family the way China treated Tan's family? It was unethical, uncaring and totally wrong. He would make sure the world heard about this; it was not going to be forgotten, nor would it go away. He would win a sympathy vote for this family, and who knew where it would end? This was a human rights issue, but China wouldn't recognise it as such.

Chen waited patiently for the horn to blast, letting him know he had arrived in Osaka. In five minutes, he would be safely in his adopted country. All his fears would vanish and stronger ideas for his criticism of China would emerge. He couldn't wait to tell Lan Mei and the professor what had happened, although his thoughts on Tan's family would never leave him; it was a ghost that would not go away, and in fact it would haunt him forever. Marcel would be at the ferry terminal to pick him up and drive him to the train station. For this Chen was very grateful, because as he had mentioned on their last train trip, the further away from the Chinese border the better.

There was the trusted Marcel waiting for him. Already he had his hand extended to shake Chen's, as he was secretly pleased he had made it back in one piece. He did harbour deep fears for his safety. "You look warn out, my friend," stated Marcel. When Chen quickly ran through the past few days, he understood why. "Let's get you to the station. I have booked you into a sleeper carriage, so climb into bed and sleep well, my friend." They didn't have much time to spare before the train arrived. Marcel handed him his ticket, shook his hand and he climbed aboard. Only another several hours and he would be home. Between now and then there was a lot of thinking to do. At the other end, Lan Mei and the professor were excited at the thought of seeing Chen again, hoping he was on time and that all went well. It seemed like he had been away for months instead of ten days. They wondered how it all panned out, and whether he had met Tan's wife and given her the money. All would be revealed when he arrived back.

"There he is, Professor, there's Chen," yelled Lan Mei as the train pulled into the station. She saw him through the carriage window. He waved to let her know he had seen her. She was so excited. "Come, Professor, I will push you down the platform and we will meet him." The professor was just as happy to see Chen as she was.

Suddenly he appeared. "He looks tired and sad," she whispered to the professor, who wholeheartedly agreed. "Oh, how we have missed you my darling," were the first words Lan Mei spoke. He took her in his arms and tears of joy ran down his face. "Lan Mei, you are my strength and my best friend ever," he told her. Then he shook the professor's hand. The professor was happy as his two 'children' were together again and for this he was truly grateful.

Over the following days Chen related all that had happened. There were tears all round, but anger, too: how could any country display such contempt towards its citizens? Fancy separating a family when they had already suffered the loss of their father. What of the children, where were they, now their mother was taken from them? Did compassion feature in this equation? Apparently not! It took Chen nearly a week to regain his strength and to clear his mind and focus on what was happening around the world. Death rates were soaring and because the virus had mutated, several new strains were still playing havoc in some countries. Where was it all going to end? Vaccines were coming on board and were now available in several countries, so was this the long-awaited saviour? Only time would tell.

For a short period, the news was all about the American elections. Mr Trump was ousted, but he did not accept this lightly and told the world that the election was rigged. He was like a spoilt child; it took him a long time to come to terms with the fact that he was unpopular and had lost. No more accusations directed at China were forthcoming from him.

The rest of the world were hot on the trail of China, though. Since the live talkshow, a storm was brewing. Demand was nearing fever pitch for Chen, Lan Mei and the professor to return for their next show. The studio was inundated with calls, all wanting the talkshow to start, but Lan Mei had to ask them to hold off until Chen was available, and once this happened there would be no holding back! The American talkshow host flew from Tokyo to Nagoya to meet with them. They hosted him at the professor's home. After having spoken with Chen on his trip back to China, he was eager for this to go to air straight away, to let the world know what was happening behind closed doors in that country. But for the professor to fly to Tokyo was an almost impossible task and now that they knew the bullet that had paralysed him was from an assassin who had been hired from China to take out the professor, this was putting everyone at risk. Another worry was the fact that the whistle-blower had once again escaped Chinese authorities and was now back in Japan; this would anger the Chinese no end. The American host could see it would be impossible to supply the needed security for these three people, so he would arrange for the talkshow to take place right here in the professor's home. He would fly his crew out, and they would set up in this house. No-one would know where the show was to be held, only the date would be known, as this had to be kept secret even to the viewers. It was arranged for a week's time.

The time had arrived, everything was set up and the show was about to go live. Three … two… one … live on air. "I would like to introduce my three speakers. Sadly the professor couldn't join us last time as he had been shot on his way to the studio and is now confined to a wheelchair. But we do have an update on how your donations were spent, as Chen has just arrived back from China. I will leave it up to you, Chen. Please take it away." "Good day everyone, as our host has mentioned, I have just arrived back in Japan after several harrowing days in China." He then went on to tell his story about Tan's family, how he so wanted to help them, but instead he divided them, which has left him devastated. "I don't know what has happened to the children at this stage, but I have someone who is trying to find out for me. It is not easy to get information from the authorities, as everything is covered up, and the outside world must know nothing. But I want you all to know the money you have donated has gone to the families who lost their breadwinners by being injected with the deadly virus. It was the company Lan Mei and I worked for, so we feel a deep sadness for these families. Life has not changed in China; they would have the world believe otherwise, but this is not true. If we hadn't found the professor, none of this would have come out in the open, so to him we are truly grateful." They then answered more questions from the host before the interview ended.

"Thank you, guys, and you, Professor, for allowing us to do our show today. I am sure there will be plenty of feedback from today's talk, as people are angry with China, and hold them responsible for the many deaths that have occurred worldwide. I will let you know the outcome from your talk tomorrow night." The crew packed up their gear and put it into their vans, as they were flying out that night. They had to be back at the studio to take all the calls that they were expecting from this show.

The next afternoon the phone rang and it was the talkshow host. He was elated, as their phones had not stopped ringing since the interview aired, their computers were inundated with e-mails and donations were coming in thick and fast for the trust. Chen's talk had hit the listeners where it hurt most and that was deep in their hearts. The ante against China was building. How long were people going to take this for? The listeners wanted Chen to come back on air and tell them if or when he had any news of Tan's family. This was the largest audience the show had attracted for many years, simply because it had affected the whole world, as everyone somewhere had lost a loved one to this deadly virus. Then he went on to say one of his crew that had visited the professor's house had since tested positive for the virus, and he had to let them know so they could be tested. He felt really bad about this, but best they knew.

After taking the Covid tests, life at the professor's home was back to normal. Lan Mei spent as much time as possible with her beloved bonsai. The professor would come out each day and spend time watching her shape the little trees, when he wasn't helping Chen put the final touch to their China project. Today they had a visit from the professor's doctor who brought with him some sad news – the professor had contracted the virus. This meant he had to self-isolate, which he agreed to do in his home surroundings. He made his bedroom his isolation hideaway and would talk to his 'children' through the door. His caregiver came every second day now to shower him, dressed in her PPE gear. A couple of days passed and the professor seemed to have trouble breathing, so this was when Chen and Lan Mei brought some PPE clothing so they could at least enter his bedroom and keep their eye on him. Chen was a broken man once again, as here was another loved one who perhaps was going to be taken from him. Why was this happening? he asked himself. It all came back to his denounced country and the virus; they were both robbing him of all that ever mattered.

The day had come for their final goodbyes. The professor was very weak, so he called his 'children' to his bedside. He was sad he couldn't hug them, but in a faint voice he told them, "You have brought so much joy to my life; it had no meaning until I met you both. Chen, you must keep going with your story as it is your life, and dear Lan Mei, look after our bonsai. All I own is now yours. You deserve all this and more, and my solicitor will contact you. Goodbye my 'children'." He closed his eyes, never to open them again. His children cried endlessly for their beloved professor. His funeral was arranged by his solicitor on the professor's request. Two days later they were called to his office to be told "All the professor owned, his house, his flat and investments now belong to you both. You are the beneficiaries of his will. He has a lot of money in his bank which has now been transferred to your account. He loved you both dearly, so enjoy all that you have." But to them, all this meant nothing without the professor. It would take a long time before they fully understood what they had been gifted, as days of mourning followed.

The talkshow host contacted them and expressed his sadness, as he had also lost two of his crew to the virus. The studio was still being inundated with donations for the trust. He suggested another live show be planned in the future, so they could personally thank all the donors for their kindness. Listeners were enquiring whether any news had surfaced about Tan's children, but alas nothing was forthcoming. Days of nothingness passed; Chen and Lan Mei were still suffering from the loss of their mentor.

A couple of nights later the phone rang and it was Lanying. "Hello, Chen, I have some news for you. Tan's children are in a home waiting for someone to foster them, until their mother is released from jail, but no-one wants three children. I would love to care for them, but I don't have the means. I would not use the trust money as it is to be used on specific families." "What do you need, Lanying, just tell us?" "I would need money for clothes as theirs were in the house when it was bulldozed down, and for beds and bedding, then I would have to feed and care for them," she told him. Chen told her to get the children and he and Lan Mei would pay all their related costs along with an allowance to her for taking the children on. "But, Chen, you can't afford that." He explained they had been gifted an inheritance from the professor and he would be thrilled to know his money was helping save children. If

Chen had one wish left, it would be to help save Tan's children, and now his wish was looking like it could come true. Perhaps life was taking a turn for the best. "Keep me informed, Lanying. Ring me when you have the children and we will send you money. You have made our day, thank you!" This would give Chen and Lan Mei a renewed interest to carry on. They would become the sponsors of Tan's children. When their mother was released, they would care for her and her family, and they would never want again. Here their sadness would end. This brought light to Chen's heart; at last he could see a positive outcome from a dark chapter in his life.

When he finished on the phone, he related it all to Lan Mei. "Oh, Chen, I'm so happy, I would have taken the children, but with the virus and the lockdown that would be impossible. Now that we have money, we can afford to help others. How nice for the children to return to the area they know. They will still have school friends there, and maybe they will be able to go back to their school and pick up where they left off. I'm so happy for them and for you, as I know this means so much to you." This was the first time since they had lost their mentor that a bright spot had appeared in their lives. With not being able to have children of her own, Lan Mei was excited at the thought of becoming involved with Tan's family, and maybe they could come to Japan for holidays. Perhaps it was time to move on and finish their research.

17

THE FALLOUT

IN THE DAY'S newspapers Chen read where Beijing continues to withhold vital information that scientists need to protect the world from this deadly virus, and the ones that may follow. United States officials stepped up their attacks on China over the pandemic, claiming they had explosive new evidence that proved Covid-19 leaked from the laboratory. It was also noted by their intelligence agencies that scientists at the Xihun laboratory fell ill in the autumn of 2019 with symptoms consistent with Covid-19, earlier than previously believed. Another story took his eye: an article recalling the death in February 2020 of a young Chinese doctor, one of the eight whistle-blowers punished by the authorities for spreading rumours on social media about a SARS-like virus, as he wanted to warn others. This sealed his peril, for going against official messaging in China. It was not long after this he fell ill with the virus and died. His death was a sensitive topic! Did he in fact meet the same fate as the poo-bin lads? Chen had his opinions on this.

Chen and the professor's project was finished and this is what their analysis shed light on … China didn't deserve a place in the future world!

China was on its own; it was now a country no-one wanted a part of. It was abandoned by the Western world because of its manufactured virus that had caused so many deaths. People had had enough, and now the time had come to punish that country for weakening the rest of the world and the global economy, for its own gain, to become the 'one and only' superpower.

This wasn't going to be an easy ride for any country, and all eyes would be on China to make sure no more viruses would be released outside of that country. The death rate would fall, but the fallout in other ways would have a huge impact, especially on the younger generation. No more Chinese imports of computers, PlayStations, iPads, cell phones, and the like and household whiteware and clothing would have to be sourced elsewhere. It may indeed make the big companies move out of China and back to their countries of origin. But this would mean a rise in prices, because no-one in the Western world would work for the meagre salaries paid to the poor of China. On the brighter side employment would rise if these big companies came back to their homelands.

But what of the food chain? This would hurt both America and China. America would have to source markets elsewhere, and China would have to live on rice and wheat and whatever else they could source in their own country. They were people rich but land poor, with comparatively little beef, fish, dairy or soy beans available to them. Governments of other countries would clamp down on Chinese land ownership, if indeed they were thinking of growing food in other countries to feed their own in China – that would not be a happening thing.

Imagine a world without cell phones, iPads and so on. The younger generation would have to adjust to a new way of life. Perhaps it would be too much of a sacrifice for them; how would they cope? They would have to learn to communicate with people rather than with cell phones. But the world would be virus free! The word 'superpower' would vanish and we would all go back to living a near to 'normal' life. Here the virtual world would end and the real world would begin once again!

The professor's solicitor arranged for the trust money to be transferred to Toshi's many bank accounts in China. This was to protect it from being tracked by Chinese authorities. She would then get the cash to Lanying, so it would be untraceable. She was a smart businesswoman and knew all the loopholes available, as she had outsmarted the Chinese authorities for years, and would continue to do so. Chen and Lan Mei would never give up their fight for the protection of Chinese citizens whose family members were deliberately injected with the virus. Many had died and those families remaining were struggling. No-one received any help whatsoever from the authorities, because they portrayed Covid as a natural virus. This is what they wanted the rest of the world to believe. Until one day a brave man from Japan, a Nobel

Prize winner in Medicine, delved into the darkness that surrounded this pandemic. And circulated a paper that happened to reach the hands of someone in China, who was just as passionate and brave, to prove the professor's findings were indeed true.

To think the professor succumbed to the actual virus that he had fought so hard to expose and bring out in the open. This was a sad irony. But in the end, his fight was not in vain, his battle had been won, China was out on a limb, and its world domination ended here!

In Chen and Lan Mei's hearts, there was a special place for the forgotten poo-bin lads who, unknowingly, gave up their lives to spread the deadly virus to many countries around the world. None of these lads knew the reason of their mission; they were used as guinea pigs by the pharmaceutical company to weaken the health and wealth of the outside world. And the professor, who formed an everlasting friendship with two complete strangers, had the evidence to show truly how, where and why the virus began.

18

LIFE MUST GO ON

WITH THE PROFESSOR GONE, it was up to Chen to carry on. Among the professor's papers he found a letter addressed to himself, stating that he must not give up, to box on and not let their findings be forgotten. Chen and Lan Mei had been deeply affected by his passing. One day ran into the next until they realised three months had passed, and it was now time to pull together and move on with life. They had been left a small fortune, something they had not thought about as this was all new to them. Their years of poverty were over and a new era had emerged, but they were still the same unassuming couple; nothing would ever change that! What had been the professor's now belonged to them, and for this they felt humbled and honoured.

Lan Mei had immersed herself in the glasshouse amid the bonsai trees, thus helping her to overcome her suffering, as she knew the professor's spirit was always there with her. It was like losing her father all over again. When Chen could not find her, he knew where to go. He would stand at the glasshouse door and hear her talking away to the professor as if he had never left. This would bring tears to his eyes. While in their mourning, they had forgotten to contact Lanying in China to see if she had custody of Tan's children, but now was the time!

Chen picked up the phone to speak with Lanying, waiting patiently to hear her voice. "Hi, Lanying, how are you? Do you have the children? You haven't asked for any money." "Oh, Chen, I am still waiting, as every time I go to get them a new block has been put in the way. They are sad little children, always asking for their mother; it makes me want to cry. I am worried about Zian; he just sits and stares into space. I have been told I can collect them at the weekend so I am hoping this time they can come home with me." Chen was angry that they were still in care. "Please ring me when you have picked them up. I will deposit money into your bank, as they must have items that will make them happy. You will know what they need. Have you had any news on their mother?" Lanying explained that no-one had heard a word. They hoped she was being treated fairly, but this could have been far from the truth, and only time would tell. On this sad note the call ended.

This was the first learning curve for Chen and Lan Mei: all the money in the world couldn't make things happen faster than they normally would. Lan Mei had been contacted by the host from the talkshow to see if she would come in and talk about her recovery from the virus and finding herself sterile. This was now happening to many young women around the world … they wanted to know why. The one thing that went through her mind, and something that Chen was working on, was zero population growth. The world was heading towards being overpopulated, and the food supply would not keep up with demand, so something had to be done to stop this happening. Was this why the virus was manufactured, to take out the elderly and the weak, the non-productive sector, to make way for a new regime that would dictate to the world what would happen? All Lan Mei wanted to do at the moment was the same as Chen wanted: to find out about Tan's children, but she said in the near future she would be willing to speak to an audience. Right now, the time wasn't right.

Meanwhile Chen was busying himself with the virus fallout, keeping notes on all that was happening around the world. Third and fourth variants of the virus had emerged worldwide, leaving behind a startling death toll. Lockdowns were recurring in many countries. Vaccines were being rolled out from several big drug companies but a successful result for the whole of the world was a long way off. China was still putting out stories that the virus was a natural virus caused by bats. No-one was completely sure; nothing had been proven to the contrary, but what Chen and the professor had discovered, to them, was proof. But it was up to the people to make up their own minds on what was fact and what was fiction! It was a personal choice.

19

THE CHILDREN

LANYING WAITED PATIENTLY at the front door of the bleak-looking building that was home to the children. Today she was not allowed to enter; the children were going to be brought to her. Time ticked by slowly, and she was becoming nervous: was it going to happen, would she be taking the children home with her today? It became apparent that once again the authorities were stalling for time. She shuffled from one foot to the other as a dark thought crossed her mind: what was happening behind the closed doors? Suddenly the doors opened and two little girls were brought out by a woman in a white uniform. They stood there sobbing, and Lanying's heart was broken. She ran to the girls and took them in her arms. But where was Zian? "Where is your brother?" she asked. "We are keeping him," was the answer. "What do you mean? He is their brother; why can't he be with them?" "Just take those two and go before I change my mind," was the hostile answer. She took the children's hands, and she could see that she could lose them if she carried on with this conversation, so off they went. Two little hands clenched each of hers as they began to walk away, but the sobbing continued. When they came to a seat, Lanying asked them why were they so sad.

They rolled up their sleeves, showing her the sore part on their arm. Lanying could not believe what she saw – they had been given an injection. "When did they do this?" she asked. "Just before you came. They hurt us." Her heart missed a beat. What had been injected into them, was it the virus? Surely not! Did they not want these little girls to live, had the authorities disposed of, or done something sinister to their mother? So many questions were running through her mind: what of Zian, what was his fate? The girls had no clothes, other than what they were wearing. Lanying remembered visiting them and they were wearing uniforms, so these must have been all they owned. She wondered if she should take them shopping but decided they were more in need of cuddles, so home they went, where they could rug up on the sofa together and she could hold them in her arms. How long would she have them? Were they going to be lost to the virus? These thoughts weighed heavily in her heart. Tears ran down her face as she pondered on their future – indeed if they were going to have one – not realising she was also now in danger of catching the virus.

Lanying had brought in food she thought they might like, along with some goodies for a special treat. She did not know how they had been treated, but now was not the time to ask. Perhaps it would all come out in general conversation over the next few days. She cooked them tea, they played games until bedtime, then the stories began. They loved Lanying lying beside them on their bed reading from some children's books. It didn't take long for them to fall asleep; it had been a long day!

Now it was time to ring Chen and let him know she had the children, all but one! "Hi, Chen, I picked up the girls today, but they kept Zian. I was not allowed to bring him home." "Why not? He is their brother; did they say what was going to happen to him?" he asked angrily. "No, they just said they were going to keep him. I started to ask questions, but they told me to go before they changed their mind about the girls, so we left. There is something else I have to tell you: both the girls had been given an injection just before I collected them, and they were in tears..." "What!" he yelled. The phone went dead for a moment. "Please tell me that is not true, oh my God! What have they been given? Lanying, you must be very careful in case it was the virus. They are young and will have a better chance of survival, but you are in danger. If you start to feel unwell, please ring me straight away and I will make arrangements to bring the girls to Japan, although right now I don't know how. The authorities will take them back if you get sick, then what will happen to them? Perhaps this is what is meant to happen. Once they get you out of the way the girls are again at their mercy. I am sorry to have to tell you this, as you have been our lifeline. Do you have a close friend you can trust to disburse the trust money, to where it is meant to go, if all does not go well?" She assured Chen she would get this in place if in case the worst possible outcome happened. She would be prepared. She took a moment to pause and think, as she had not thought of the consequences to herself; all she wanted was to save her best friend's children. Chen finished by telling her he had put money into her bank, so to splash out on the girls.

When the girls woke the next morning, they still had very sore arms. On inspection they were bright red and swollen, so Lanying wrapped a frozen packet of peas in a tea-towel and applied it to the swollen areas to help take the swelling down. They had to go to the shops to get clothing and pyjamas as the girls had slept in their knickers. She let them choose the clothes they liked; God knows they deserved some enjoyment in their young lives. Some laughter was forthcoming as they tried on many different items, but they were at last having fun. Then it was on to the ice-cream shop for a treat. "We haven't had an ice-cream since Mother was taken from us," the youngest girl commented.

One week had now passed and the girls were still not healthy enough to start back at their old school. They still had aches and pains, which worried Lanying. Was this the virus working its way through their bodies? Chen had told her not to discuss the girls' injections with anyone, in case they had to instantly arrange for them to leave China. China was nearly back to normal on the virus front apart from flying, as no planes were flying passengers overseas anywhere in the world; there were just internal flights along with freight. The ferries were still sailing, but with strict rules. Lanying took particular notice of her own health, as if in fact the girls had been injected with the virus, she was in danger. She would have to make arrangements regarding the trust funds, as it had developed into a huge money earner. People around the world were still donating to Chen and Lan Mei's fight for justice for the families whose breadwinners were injected with the virus. Many families had and were still receiving monetary help, something of which, as yet, the Chinese authorities had no knowledge. It was discreetly managed, and even the recipients were unaware of the source, but that's the way it had to be and would remain.

Today the girls were on their way to school. It had been months since they had seen their friends and they were excited. Lanying took them into the school grounds where groups of children had gathered. But instead of embracing them, the girls were shunned, and no-one came forward to welcome them. Suddenly a voice rang out: "There they are. They have been locked away, and their mother is in jail". Lanying was shocked and the girls huddled together in fright. Where were their old friends? She stood in disbelief, but her instinct told her to stand up for the girls. "These are your friends, and they belong at your school. Please make them welcome." But the groups dispersed and walked away; no-one came forward! With this, Lanying took the girls' hands and walked to the school office. She told the principal what had transpired in the school grounds, and he answered, "I will try to sort this out, but we can't make children like other children." She was appalled by this answer. Were the girls ever going to be accepted? The irony of it all was that all these children's parents were receiving money that the girl's mother had administered and because of this, the authorities took her away.

The principal summoned a teacher to take the girls to a classroom to begin lessons. Lanying stood outside the school gates to see what would happen at lunch break. She was sad to see them sitting on their own, as no-one had yet befriended them. After a week of being shunned by the other children, she decided to ring Chen and explain the situation. He was disappointed and sad. "Perhaps we should look at bringing them to Japan where they would have a new beginning; how would you feel about that?" "Chen, I think that would be the best option for them. No-one wants them at their school, and it is so sad to watch. They have to be educated, but it is not working for them here." Chen told Lanying to leave it to him. He would see what he could arrange, although of course it would have to be an underground operation; the authorities must not know.

It didn't appear as if the girls were spreading the virus, so perhaps the injections had had another purpose. Would they end up sterile? Was this the continuing of a depopulation vaccine? Only time would tell. For the next month the girls attended school but failed to attract friends, and it was a nightmare for them. The saving grace was the big school holidays were about to begin. This was a joyous thought.

Meanwhile, Chen and Lan Mei were busy making plans to secretly bring the girls to Japan to begin a new life. Chen had contacted Toshi, who had arrangements under way. The risk to fly them was too great, so it would have to involve using the ferry. Now that the hype on the 'whistle-blowers' had died down, Lan Mei decided to take the ferry to China where Toshi would have the girls at the port, with all the relevant passports and visas. Then they would catch the return crossing that night. The girls knew nothing of these arrangements for fear of information being leaked. If Chinese authorities suspected what was about to happen, they would seize the girls and they would probably never be seen again! This all had to happen in the school holidays which were now beginning in China. Lan Mei would catch the train, then meet up with Marcel who would take her to the ferry. She would travel under her own passport until she reached China, then Toshi would have a forged return passport for her, as a mother with her two daughters. She had done all this before so knew what to expect.

The day had arrived. Lanying had packed a suitcase each for the girls, who were going away for a holiday. They were excited, but she was heartbroken; would she ever see the girls again? She felt she had failed her friend, but then no-one knew if she was alive. She still had Zian to think about. As she hugged them goodbye the tears flowed. "Don't cry, Aunty, we will be back soon," they reassured her. Toshi arrived on time and was introduced to the girls, who then climbed into her car. They noticed pillows and a blanket on the back seat and asked, "What are these for?" "We are going to be driving right through the night, so when you are tired you can curl up and go to sleep," answered Toshi. She gave them electronic games to play to keep them occupied. They stopped for lunch and a toilet stop. As night-time approached, they decided to stop for a meal break and their last toilet stop before settling down for the night. It didn't take long before they had dropped off to sleep. Toshi kept driving, as she had timed it so they would arrive at the port two hours before the ferry sailed. Lan Mei would be at the terminal waiting for them.

The girls stirred mid-morning and wondered where they were, as the car was still going. "Are we there yet?" they wanted to know. "We will be at the ferry terminal soon, then you can get out and stretch your legs and we will get something to eat." "I have to go to the toilet soon," said the eldest girl. "Can you hold on for another fifteen minutes? Then we will be there." "I'll try," came the answer. Toshi chattered away about the buildings, hoping the toilet thoughts would fade. Half an hour passed as they pulled up at the ferry terminal, then made their way to Toshi's office where there was a toilet.

As Toshi entered her office she noticed Lan Mei through the window so called to her. They greeted each other with a hug. She quickly explained that the girls knew nothing about going to Japan, and this was for their own protection. They waited for the girls to come back, then began the introductions. Lan Mei felt an instant bond with the girls; they were the daughters she could never have. "Now girls, you are going to be sailing to Japan with Lan Mei, and while on the ferry you must call her 'Mother'. Please don't ask questions, as all will be explained when you get to Japan. Now let us find a place to eat." During the meal Lan Mei observed the girls. They were well mannered but as yet were still very quiet, and she could understand why, as they had been through so much. "We didn't know we were going to Japan for a holiday. That's a long way," said the youngest. "You will love it there as you will be staying with my partner and me. I grow bonsai trees in a big glasshouse." "What are they?" Lan Mei explained that, like them, she knew nothing about them before going to Japan to live, so explained what they were. The girls smiled, fancy growing trees in a bowl? The ice was broken and the questions started.

Time had come to get the suitcases out of the car. They only had fifteen minutes to board the ferry as the first horn had blasted. Lan Mei was given the passports with their visas for the girls, so they bade farewell to Toshi and headed for the gangway. It was only then that the girls noticed that Lan Mei dragged her leg; what was wrong? they wondered. Lan Mei knew her way around the ferry so after they went through Customs, she looked for their cabin. As she was making her way to the appropriate deck, she noticed a police officer looking at her. Suddenly she felt sick; it was the officer that had befriended her on her last journey. Did he recognise her? She quickly unlocked the cabin door and went inside, followed by the girls. They each picked their beds, then asked Lan Mei if she was happy with the one she was left with. "Yes, my pets, that's fine with me. We will be on the ferry for two nights, then when we get to Tokyo we will catch the overnight train to Nagoya. You will be really exhausted by the time we get home, but it will be a wonderful experience for you both." "Gosh, we are lucky. Who is paying for all this?" asked the eldest child. "Chen and I wanted to shout you this holiday. Now let me get your names right. You, being the eldest, your name is Ling and you, the youngest, are Shui. I will have to remember these names, but tell me if I get them mixed up." After this, they all collapsed onto their beds ready for a rest. The girls talked among themselves, while Lan Mei lay quiet with her eyes closed listening to what they were saying. They seemed happy enough. Then they mentioned their mother, wondering when she was coming home. "I wish Zian was here. He would love this," said Ling. "I hope they don't hurt him any more; he was sad when we had to leave. Do you think they will let him go home with aunty one day?" asked Shui.

After resting for an hour, the girls asked, "Can we go out on the deck and watch the waves?" "I will come with you. I don't want anything to happen to either of you while we are on the ferry," Lan Mei told them. With this they each put on a coat before they left the cabin. As they made their way on to the deck, Lan Mei hoped with all her heart that she would not meet the officer. What did he know? It was months since her image had been made public, she reassured herself, so surely, he wouldn't remember? The girls stood close to Lan Mei and climbed on the first wire of the rail, but they soon dismounted as the sea was tossing and flinging the waves hard against the side of the ferry, covering them with spray. It looked angry; was this a warning? "Do you think we had better go to our cabin?" asked Shui. It was as if she had a bad feeling. Had the waves stirred up her thoughts? "Yes, pets, let's leave the sea to its own anger. We will get something to eat at the cafeteria, then have an early night."

As they sat in the café waiting for their food to arrive, there he was! Lan Mei tried to hide behind the girls, but she had been spotted and over he came. "Hello, we meet again. Where have you been this time?" he asked. She was speechless, and panic set in. Did he remember her from her image? So many thoughts flashed through her mind; what would she say, was her world about to come crashing down? A little voice broke the silence, "Mother, what's wrong?" Ling remembered she had to call Lan Mei 'Mother' while on the ferry. Lan Mei was still trying to gather her composure, and she had to find out what he knew. "It's alright pet. Perhaps we can meet tomorrow," she said as she addressed the officer. "I'm off duty tomorrow night. Meet me here, same time, same place! See you then, I'm looking forward to that," he said in a tone that made her feel uncomfortable. This made her feel he definitely knew something, but what?

After playing a few games, the girls decided to get some sleep. They fell asleep as soon as their heads hit the pillow; it had been a big day for them. Lan Mei, on the other hand, had a terrible night, and she had tossed and turned wondering what was going to be said when she met the officer. She wondered if she should carry a weapon of sorts, to protect herself. It was a big bad world out there; this she had experienced! Chen had packed a letter opener, a knife with a long thin blade, which he thought would go undetected, but if questioned it was explainable. She would tuck it in her sock, which would be concealed by her long pants, when she went to meet the officer. The girls slept well into the next morning so Lan Mei made the call to combine breakfast and lunch all in one, and off to the cafeteria they went. They were able to find a table by a window, allowing them to view the sea. Today it was calm; it must have shed its anger during the night and woken up in a better mood. The girls commented on the sea's behaviour. "We were frightened last night on deck, but it looks so friendly today. Can we go out on deck after we have eaten?" Lan Mei agreed and told them they would try to spot some whales and dolphins. Thus, an enjoyable afternoon was spent and several dolphins were seen swimming alongside the ferry. The girls decided they would like to take some sandwiches back to the cabin for tea, so they could continue with their games.

The time had come for Lan Mei to meet the officer, as per last night's arrangement. She told the girls she would be back soon, not to leave the cabin or open the door to anyone other than herself. They would use a secret knock. She felt nervous; what was going to unfold? It was dark as she made her way along the deck, then suddenly there he was!

In the officer's mind, he had a picture of Lan Mei declining his offer of help, all those months ago, letting him know that even though she was a cripple, she was independent and didn't need him. He had harboured a sensual thought about this strong-minded girl, then when he found out who she was, his thoughts of collecting the reward had slipped through his fingers. But today his situation was different. Hard times had befallen him, he had lost his wife to the virus, and now the money would benefit him immensely. This was a big chance to change his life. He could take from her, as well as capitalise on the small fortune. Tonight, he would have his way with her, then hand her over to the authorities. Would she still be full of fight? This he longed to experience, and the thought excited him.

"Hello again!" he greeted her. "Come with me, I want to talk to you," and he led her to the back of the ferry to a secluded seat. He knew there were no security cameras in this area, so it would be his word against hers. "What have you been up to in Japan? I heard there were two whistle-blowers who left China. Do you know anything about them?" he asked. This took Lan Mei completely by surprise. What was he thinking, and why did he ask this? She was lost for words. "Come, my pretty, I know who you are, and if I hand you over to the authorities, I stand to make a lot of money. Perhaps I could take the reward out in favours." He placed his hands on her knee, then started to move them up towards her groin. "Don't touch me!" she warned him. "I liked your courage right from our first meeting. I see you still have that fight in you," and with this he grabbed her and pulled her hard against him. Excitement was racing through his veins; his body was responding and she could feel his manly part pressing into her. Fear took over; could she reach the knife? No, she would have to free herself first. She struggled trying to fight him off and managed to break free from his embrace, but not his clutches. Now could she reach the knife? She leaned sideways – yes, she grasped it and plunged it into his chest. "You bitch," he yelled as he lurched forward. She was in survival mode and knew she had to finish him off, otherwise her life was over. She stabbed him several times until he lay still and silent. In the darkness she dragged him over to the rail then pushed him under the bottom wire and watched as he disappeared into the dark abyss. She took off her jacket and wiped the deck in case any blood had seeped through his clothing, then threw the jacket and the paper knife into the sea. She looked around to see there were no witnesses to what had just happened. She felt alone and frightened. Once again, she had committed a murder, not by choice but in self-defence. She burst into tears, as she was not a person who was out for revenge, but now that she had two little girls to love and protect, survival was paramount. She sat down on the seat to regain her composure before she returned to the cabin. Her nightmare was over, but could she forget what happened tonight? When would the officer be missed? What was going to surface from his disappearance? Lan Mei would just have to wait and see! Tomorrow they would be on the train on their way home to Nagoya.

On returning to the cabin, she found Ling and Shui sound asleep cuddled up together in Ling's bed, and this is where Lan Mei left them. This allowed her time to have a shower and reflect on the night's happenings. If luck was on her side, nothing would be discovered before they left the ferry. She was woken by the girls who had climbed into her bed; she felt the closeness of their bodies. "Good morning, pets," she mumbled in a sleepy voice. Suddenly a horn sounded and Lan Mei knew this meant they were about to berth. "Come, girls, we have to get dressed and packed, as we have arrived." What a scramble. Breakfast was off the menu, and hunger would have to suffice until they were on the train. She had to get off the ferry, then hopefully what happened last night would just be a distant memory. She had learned in her short life thus far that sometimes compassion had to be overridden by something just as important ... called survival! "Hurry, girls, we are going to be met by Marcel when we leave the ferry, and he will drive us to the train station. This will be the last leg of our journey, then we will be home."

Now they were settled into their sleeping compartments after having eaten hamburgers and chips at the station, before boarding the train. It was a long night ahead, but Lan Mei couldn't wait to see Chen again; she missed him. What would he think of the girls? She knew now their life was complete, but for one little hiccup, Zian!

20

COMING HOME

THE GIRLS WOKE to the blast of the train horn. As they stirred, they realised they were still fully dressed, as this was the way they had snuggled into their beds in a tired state last night. "Are we there?" they asked. "Yes, my pets, climb down then we will push the beds back into the wall. Another ten minutes and you will meet Chen. He will love you both. We never had children of our own, so we will pretend you are our children." "But what about Mother, will we ever see her again?" asked Ling. Lan Mei told the girls she hoped it wouldn't be too long and they would be reunited as a family, but in the meantime, she wanted them to be happy. "Our old friends didn't like us at school when we came back. I'm glad we are on holiday," Shui replied. Lan Mei cuddled the girls. They had no idea what was in store for them.

Chen was waiting on the station platform. He had missed Lan Mei, and it was going to be great to have her back home with him, along with two extra girls. All the money in the world meant very little without his love beside him. It was together they had won the heart of the professor, thus ending up in the very privileged situation that they now found themselves. In their wildest dreams they could not have envisaged this happening to them. But during many conversations they came to the same conclusion: in their hearts they knew they had to help and protect Tan's children from a life of mere existence. They deserved more, for the heartache they had suffered was not of their own doing but was due to the country and its harsh system. They could never bring Tan back and God knows what had happened to the children's mother; would they ever see her again? Chen blamed himself for the children being taken from their mother, but all the guilt in the world could not change the past. It was in the now they had to live; the past was gone forever! Suddenly the train was in view … only a few more minutes, then it would pull up at the platform and he would feel Lan Mei's arms around him once again.

"There he is girls. There's Chen," yelled Lan Mei. She ran to him and put her arms around him, holding on for dear life, where she felt safe and comforted. "I've missed you," she whispered in his ear. Then she remembered the girls and introduced them. "Come and meet Chen. … Chen, this is Ling and Shui." He reached for their hands. "Welcome to Japan, girls, you will love it here; the people are so friendly and polite. You will be bowed to on every meeting, so it is customary to return the bow. Come, our driver is waiting, and you must be tired after all your travelling." They smiled at Chen. Lan Mei took the girls' hands while Chen put the suitcases on a trolley, which he wheeled out to a waiting car, where a driver awaited them. He opened the car doors and bowed to the girls. This brought on a burst of the giggles. To have a car driven by someone else and the doors opened for them along with the customary bow just added to the excitement. Lan Mei climbed into the back seat with the girls, who were still suffering from the giggles. They had never seen such strange behaviour; this was certainly a different country to the one they were used to. Like Lan Mei, they were astounded by the lack of poverty seen while driving to where they were going. "Look at those funny-shaped tiny trees in pots," yelled Shui. "That was the first thing I noticed when I came to Japan. They are the bonsai trees I was telling you about. I grow them in a big glasshouse; you will love them. I will teach you all about them," she told them.

As they entered the driveway to their home, the girls were in disbelief. "Where are we?" they asked. "We are home; this is where we live, and it will be your home too, for however long it takes," Lan Mei explained. As the driver alighted and opened the car doors for the girls he bowed once again, thus more giggles followed. "What is that?" asked Ling as she pointed to the glasshouse. Lan Mei took them over and opened the door, and there before them were shelves filled with the funny little trees in pots. "These are my bonsai. They belonged to the professor; we both shared a love for them, but he passed away. I spend many hours in here." The girls walked around inspecting them, laughing and chatting away to themselves. "We love them too; can we learn how to grow them?" they asked. "Yes, my pets, I will teach you all you want to know. Now come, we will get you settled into our home."

Several hours had passed and the girls were settled into their bedroom. Their clothes had all been hung up or put into drawers. They had never seen such luxury, and this was starting to show as the excitement was building. The house was large and the grounds were huge, as the lawns and gardens seemed to stretch for miles. As Lan Mei passed the bedroom, she overheard them talking. Ling said to Shui, "We are so lucky we have come for a holiday to a palace. Lan Mei must be very rich. I like her; she is so kind, she is like a mother." This brought tears to her eyes. It was her dearest wish to give Chen children, but it was never going to happen; now she had two little girls who thought she was like a mother. She went to find Chen and tell him what she had just heard. The tears were still sitting in her eyes, shining like diamonds, and a maternal feeling overcame her. She wanted to hold Chen and make love to him, then it would all feel real!

Lan Mei cooked several Japanese dishes for dinner so the girls could have a choice. It was not so much different to Chinese food apart from the sushi and different spices. They were not hard to please, as poverty had taught them that any food was better than no food. They chattered all through the meal, asking questions about all sorts of things, thus making Lan Mei feel they were settling in; in other words, being themselves – two little girls who were enjoying life. After dinner, when the dishes were all cleaned up and put away, Chen decided to turn on the television to listen to the news. They all squeezed together on the settee like a typical family. Suddenly an image came on the screen that made the girls yell, "We know that man. He talked to you at our table, remember, when we were on the ferry?" Lan Mei went into shock. She had put all that behind her, thinking it would never surface again, but there it was, the cold hard facts were indeed there. The news spokesperson carried on: 'We are appealing to a mother and her two children who were aboard the ferry going to Japan on Wednesday, 12 May to come forward. All other passengers have been contacted. Now we are asking this mother to make contact with the relevant authorities. The police officer who is missing is presumed to have fallen overboard. We are looking for any unusual behaviour that may have been seen by any passengers. Officer Lu had been chief officer aboard the ferry for several years, so this incident is being treated as suspicious. Divers at this moment are searching the sea, as it is known when the officer was last seen by his colleges.' "You know him Lan Mei. Remember, he came over to our table," insisted Shui. Lan Mei panicked; how much did the girls remember?

Even Chen remembered his face from their last voyage. "You had better contact the police," he told her. "I can't, Chen. You knew we were travelling on false passports to get the girls safely out of China. We just have to ignore this. We can't risk any disclosure of the girls' whereabouts." Chen agreed, as for a moment he had forgotten the secrets they were harbouring. "Why don't people know we are in Japan?" asked Ling after hearing this conversation. "We will discuss this tomorrow, as you have had a big day. Now it is time to shower and get ready for bed." "Did you speak with him on the ferry?" asked Chen. Lan Mei signalled to him not to pursue this subject any further. Was she going to tell Chen the truth or a lie? It was not in her nature to hide secrets from him; he was her lover and her best friend, but another murder, how was he going to handle that? Knowing Chen, he would understand when he knew it was in self-defence, as she was very dear to him. Lan Mei was forced to take such action when it meant being raped then handed over to the authorities.

After tucking the girls up in bed, Lan Mei told them the story about the professor and how they became beneficiaries of his estate, and all that was his was now theirs. "Gosh, he must have really loved you and Chen to give you all this?" said Shui. "Yes, we felt blessed and now we want to share it with people we love. That's how life works with Chen and me," then she bade them goodnight and left the room. Now to speak with Chen; how would she start the conversation? She went and sat next to him on the settee and asked him to hold her while she told what had happened. Chen sat and listened. He got uptight when he knew the officer had tried to rape Lan Mei. Of course she had to retaliate and defend herself; the officer was nothing but scum. In her panic she stabbed him, realising if she didn't finish him off, she was in danger of being put away forever. Chen held her close, and tears trickled down her cheeks as she described this dreadful incident, and all the emotions of it came flooding back. She thought she could erase it from her mind, but it was still there. "You did right, Lan Mei. Don't punish yourself. He got what he deserved; you were at a disadvantage and he used his position to intimidate you. This will be our secret along with many others. It is called self-survival and together we are survivors! Come to bed. I have missed you!"

Lan Mei couldn't wait to cuddle up to Chen; he was her hero, her comforter, her everything! She couldn't keep her hands from caressing and teasing him, and she wanted to be touched and loved in return. Chen sensed her need and was only too willing to engage in foreplay. She was his brave warrior, and he kissed and caressed her, knowing what her desires were. Her response sent him into a whirlwind of passion, and he knew this was her happy place, making love, being loved and knowing she felt equal to every other abled-bodied woman. To her, sex was an equaliser and all disabilities were discarded. While making love there were no barriers or boundaries; it was the connection of two consenting people claiming the ultimate prize!

Today the girls were up early exploring their new surroundings, eventually gravitating to the glasshouse. This was the most amazing place to them, and they had never seen anything like it before; it was as if a fairy tale had come to life. It was those funny little trees that amazed them and made them laugh, just as had happened when Lan Mei first arrived in Japan. Was this history repeating itself? Ling couldn't keep her hands off the bonsai, following their shapes, touching and smelling them and reassembling all the little stones that surrounded them in their dishes. She felt mesmerised by them, and this was her favourite place; she wished she could stay here forever. Lan Mei could hear the laughter ringing out as the girls ran around like mad hatters, trying to explore everything at the same time. 'How lovely to hear laughter. These are my girls, the ones I could never have, but by the grace of God we have been given this chance to care for and love these children.' She felt her life was complete but for one other – Zian!

21

WHAT HAPPENS NEXT

A MONTH HAD PASSED and it was as if it was yesterday when the girls arrived; where had the time gone? They had settled in, and this now felt like their home, where they were happy and wanted to stay. "How much longer can we stay?" Shui asked Chen. "When does school start?" Chen asked. The mention of school brought tears to her eyes. "I don't want to go back to school; no-one likes us any more. Can't we stay here with you forever? You and Lan Mei could be our new mother and father." This blew Chen's mind; he hadn't dared think along these lines for fear of being heartbroken if the girls had to leave. But he and Lan Mei knew the girls could never go back to China, as it would not be safe for them. If they mentioned they had been to Japan, the authorities would be on their trail, putting all four of them in danger. This was not going to happen! But how were they going to tell Ling and Shui?

School had started back in China as the big holidays

were over. That night, Chen received a phone call from Lanying, saying the authorities had been notified that the girls had not returned to school, so they came to her house demanding to know where they were. "What did you tell them?" he asked. In her panic she told them some relations had come to pick them up and as yet hadn't brought them back. "In a couple of days, ring them and pretend you are worried as they have not come back, then that will take the suspicion away from you." "That is brilliant, Chen. I have been to see Zian a couple of times, but he is so sad, he wants to be with his sisters. Next time I will ask to see if he can come and stay for a few days. Could we sneak him to Japan? He needs to be rescued. I would love to look after him, but he would suffer the same as the girls, when it came to going to school. It breaks my heart," she answered quietly. Chen told her to leave it with him. He would think of something, then if the chance arose, they would certainly try to smuggle him into Japan.

The next night Chen and Lan Mei sat the girls down to have a serious talk. Chen asked, "If you could wish for anything, what would you choose?" "We have talked and we want to live here with you and Lan Mei. We have never been so happy. We can hardly remember what our mother looks like, and we don't know if we will ever see her again, but we know she loves us. Could Zian live here with us?" they asked. Chen looked at Lan Mei, and her tears told him all he needed to know. Now it was time to tell some truths.

"Ling and Shui, we want you both to live here with us,

as you have become our children. The truth is, you cannot go back to China, because we smuggled you into Japan on false passports, and if you went there the authorities would put you back into that awful home. We have had no news of your mother so we don't know if she is still alive, but if we find her, we will bring her to Japan to be with you. One day we hope to bring Zian here, but it will not be easy." The girls leaped with joy, "Is this our new home? Can we live here forever? Oh, Lan Mei, I will be able to care for the bonsai, just like you said," shouted Ling. With this she rushed over and clung to her. Chen explained that they would have to attend school so he would enrol them in an English-speaking school which they would have to attend every day. The girls knew this would have to happen, and they hoped it would be different to what they experienced in China. It could not be worse!

In the evening, as Chen watched the late news, he learned that the police had pulled a body from the sea that was believed to be the missing officer. On examination it showed he had been stabbed several times so this had now become a homicide case. The police were still appealing for the mother and her two children to come forward; had they witnessed foul play and were they too afraid to speak with the authorities? Chen's heart went out to Lan Mei and for this reason he decided not to make mention of this, as it would just bring back memories that were best forgotten.

Chen's time had been taken up with everything other than what the professor had left him to carry on with, but now he was back in his study. In Japan, the papers were more open about world affairs than in China. The virus was still rearing its ugly head, just when it was thought to be under control in some countries, others were still suffering big time. There didn't seem to be any pattern. Vaccines were rolling out, with three companies supplying them, but each had a different storage regime, so this was causing a headache. Some countries could not store them at the very low temperature they had to be kept at, due to their isolation. This was a new beginning; the world was flying blind on the implications of how the vaccines would affect people. Some vaccines had to be applied twice before one was fully immunised. No-one knew what the future held; would the vaccines be the magic cure to wipe out the virus?

The breakaway from China had not yet eventuated. Countries were very cautious; they were weighing up the consequences, as Australia was still trying to find new markets for their produce that China refused to take. They had a surplus of wine, crayfish and beef, this was to their detriment, but to other countries' benefit. New Zealand was one of the beneficiaries as the price of crayfish soared, and they became a main supplier. Chen now saw that China was a big player in the global economy. The question was: did they release the virus to let it be known to the rest of the world they were a force to be reckoned with?

America was still in total disarray. The 'Black lives matter' campaign was stronger than ever, as shootings of African Americans were still happening, and rioting was rife as people felt their rights were being violated. Mr

Trump's departure from the White House was also controversial, as he incited his people to stand up and be counted, which they did in an unorthodox and violent way. The virus still had a strong hold in many American cities and the vaccine rollout was not as quick as was promised. Would the new president make America great again?

India was now suffering its worst bout of the virus, which was being blamed on the holy week in which thousands of people gathered in the Ganges River to celebrate. Some countries had banned Indian residents from entering their country. In Brazil more contagious variants were emerging, causing the death rate to soar to its worst-ever high. Canada was also experiencing a spike in the virus. Chen was following all countries and how the virus impacted on them. In his adopted country of Japan, the virus was still rampant too, so things could change in an instant. The world was unstable, predictions were impossible, life had to be lived day by day.

Just as well there was happiness at home, where the girls were a welcome distraction, bringing much joy to their household. They were settled into school and loving it, which was a far cry from what they had experienced in their last month of schooling in China. Tonight, as they were eating dinner, a phone call came from Lanying in China, bringing unexpected news. Her best friend, Ling and Shui's mother, had died of the virus. The authorities had contacted her asking her to have Zian for a week so she could break the news to him. "How did you get on about the girls?" asked Chen. She told him she rang the authorities, and told them she was very upset because the girls had not been returned to her, so now there was a 'watch' out for them. This had diverted any suspicion away from her. Now the door was open to get Zian out of the country. They only had a narrow time frame for this to happen, a week starting from tomorrow. The ferry was out of the question due to ongoing police investigations around the murdered officer. Flying might be an option, but who would accompany Zian? Chen knew Toshi would be able to help, as her company dealt with these matters, and it would have to be an underground arrangement. Chen told Lanying they would talk later as the girls were present, and he didn't want them to learn about their mother until he had spoken with Lan Mei. He couldn't express his sadness for the death of her best friend over the phone, for various reasons, but he would speak with her later. It was no surprise to hear Tan's wife had died, as he knew what lay in store for those who bucked the system. Thank God they had rescued the girls. Now it was an all-out effort to bring Zian to Japan … but how?

"Hi Toshi, this is Chen, I have just had a call from Lanying who has been granted charge of Zian for a week, to break the news that his mother has died. This is our window to get him out of China. Can you help? Cost is irrelevant." "Chen, I have arranged for a family to come to Japan on a freight ship on Monday. It is not sailing into Tokyo but to a little-known port further south. Leave it to me. I'll arrange something, and I'm sure another passenger won't be a worry; perhaps he could be an added member of the family. I will be back to you as soon as it is arranged." The next big decision was how and when they were going to tell the girls their mother had passed away. The girls had not talked about her much lately, as there was too much going on in their lives.

Tonight was the night to talk to the girls. After dinner they were asked to sit at the table, which made them wary that something was up for discussion. Chen had asked Lan Mei to break the sad news to them, as he felt she was much more sensitive than him; she definitely had a soft way with children. "Ling and Shui, Lanying rang to tell us your mother contracted the virus and has passed away. Chen and I are so sad this has happened, as we hoped you would all be able to meet again, but remember one thing, your mother loved you both dearly. Please keep this thought in your hearts." The girls looked at her and she could see the tears forming, then they flowed uncontrollably. "We are so sad for Mother, she will miss us," sobbed Shui, who was the younger. Ling sat in silence; it was confronting to be told this, it was something she never wanted to hear. She was so sure she would see her mother again, but this was not to be. "Just as well we have you to love us, Lan Mei. You can be our new mother," sobbed Shui. Ling got up from the table and left the room to go outside. Chen followed her as she headed to the glasshouse, where she opened the door and cried out loud, calling to her mother in a high-pitched voice. Chen's heart was broken as he witnessed her grief pouring out. He knew it had to come out, otherwise she would store it inside then become sick. He left her to work through her grief and went back to find Lan Mei, as he felt she was needed. As he entered the dining room, he found Shui sobbing in Lan Mei's arms. It was a sad time for these young girls; they had lost both their parents. "Lan Mei, please go to Ling. She is in the glasshouse and she needs you. I will look after Shui." As Chen sat down Shui came and sat next to him.

Lan Mei ran to the glasshouse to be there for Ling. She found her sitting on a bench with her head in her hands crying out loud. "Come, Ling, let me hold you. I love you and Shui; you are the daughters I never had, but I have been so blessed that you came into my life. Both Chen and I will love you and care for you. I will never take your mother's place, but we will make her proud of her girls." Ling lifted her head and looked at Lan Mei. "Thank you, you have been so kind, and we are happy living here with you and Chen; we feel this is our home. I just feel guilty that we were so happy when mother was dying and we never knew. I know she loved us, and I will get over this in time." "We don't expect you not to grieve; it is part of losing someone dear to you. Let it take as long as it needs," Lan Mei told her. "Come inside with me, as Chen has something that will help you through this grief."

They walked into the house hand in hand to join Shui and Chen. Lan Mei told Chen to tell the girls some good news. With this he told them they were working on bringing Zian to Japan to join them and how it could happen. They were just waiting on final confirmation from Toshi. He told them that like their departure from China, it had to be done secretly so that the Chinese authorities would know nothing until it was all over and by then it would be too late. The girls were surprised and pleased to hear this, as they would be together again as a family. "Mother will be happy to know we will be a family again," said Shui. Ling, who was two years older, took the situation much closer to her heart.

The next night a call came through from Toshi to say all was on track. She had talked to Lanying, who would pick Zian up from her home and drive him to the port that the freight ship was departing from. The ship was leaving late at night so the family was in hiding until dark, when Zian would join them. It would take two nights to cross the sea, then Marcel would meet them and smuggle them in his van to a little town further up the coast. It was then up to Chen and his driver to meet them and pick up Zian. When Chen told Ling and Shui that it was all go, it brought smiles to their faces. Life was slowly returning to normal, and Lan Mei talked openly to the girls about their mother, as she was never to be forgotten. The only worry for Chen was what was going to happen to Lanying when Zian was to be returned to the authorities. Would they smell a rat? He needed to ring her and discuss how she was going to handle it.

Chen rang the following morning. "Lanying, what are you going to tell the authorities when they come to pick up Zian?" "Please don't worry about me. I have just found out I have the virus. I haven't been well for the last two days and it was confirmed today. I have to isolate and wait to see what happens. If I don't get better don't worry, as I feel I have honoured my friend's friendship by helping to reunite her family. They will have a wonderful life with you and Lan Mei. This is my dearest wish fulfilled." This was a terrible shock to Chen; what could he say? "Don't feel bad, Chen, I have entrusted the trust money to a reliable person, and she will ring you if anything happens. Just one thing: Zian was given an injection before he came to me. I have no idea what it was; his arm was still sore when Toshi picked him up." A sudden chill flowed through Chen's body; is this how Lanying got the virus? He dared not mention anything to her; perhaps it was better that she didn't know. Chen asked her if he could do anything to help. Lanying told him he had been more than generous to her, affording her a life in the last year that she could only have dreamed of. On this sad note they bade their farewells, agreeing to be in touch when Zian arrived safely in Japan. Now he had to tell Lan Mei about Lanying, but he would keep it from the girls, as they didn't need any more bad news.

Everyone was on edge as the next three days passed. They had no contact with the ship or any information as to its name or destination, for security reasons. The only news would be forthcoming from Marcel, when the ship berthed at the unknown port.

The girls were getting excited about seeing their brother, and they knew he would love living with Chen and Lan Mei. It would take him a little while to settle, as he had difficulty adjusting to any new situation. He missed his father; he was his buddy and he had never got over his death. Sadly, Tan was not around to see his children growing up, all because his brother cut his life short. Little did Chen know when he started his job at the pharmaceutical company all those years ago that he would be father to Tan's children. The strange thing was, they were never really close friends, just workmates. One day he would tell the children how he met their father. The third day had arrived and everyone was eager for the phone to ring for news on Zian. But as midnight approached there was still no call; surely nothing had gone wrong? Just before he climbed into bed, Chen told Lan Mei he had a bad feeling; he didn't know why but the feeling lingered.

The next morning, he was woken by the phone ringing, so he jumped up and answered it. "Hello Chen, Marcel here. Something has happened on the ship. Some of the crew and most of the passengers have the virus, so the ship is not allowed to berth. It has to stay at sea for fourteen days. This has posed a big problem for us, as all passengers including our undercover ones have to be tested by the port authorities before they disembark at the end of that time. I have been in touch with Toshi and we are trying to figure out how to handle this. It has never happened before so this is new territory for us. I will keep you posted when any news comes to light. Bye for now!" Chen felt sick. Up until now everything had gone to plan, but he did have that sinking feeling in his heart that all was not well. His first thought immediately now went to Zian. Was he injected with the virus? Is that how Lanying and now the people on the ship caught the virus? Was this a repeat of what had happened to his work colleagues? Did the authorities suspect something strange when the girls were not returned to Lanying? Was this a strategy set up to catch her out? So many questions swirled around in Chen's mind. Had his and Lan Mei's luck run out? He knew from experience that life threw curve balls along the way; was this one? Lan Mei heard all this as she lay beside Chen in their bed. "Do you think the authorities are suspicious, and that's why they injected Zian? Perhaps this is their way of finally breaking Tan's family bubble, so no-one is left to question what has happened. If this is the case, they are guilty as sin, but of course we have known this all along. How we survived is a miracle, although it wasn't without its challenges; it makes me shudder to think back. I suppose all we can do is wait until we hear from Marcel or Toshi. The girls will be disappointed."

The next report from Marcel brought some alarming news. The ship's captain did not want to be caught with unlawful passengers aboard, as this spelt disaster for him – he could lose his job! He told those who had no passports they would have to jump overboard and swim to shore in the darkness of the night. "But he can't do that!" said an irate Chen. "He accepted underhand payments to deliver Zian." Marcel told Chen that when the chips were down and someone's head was going to roll, there was no such thing as compassion; it was all for one's self. "How far out to sea is the ship anchored?" he asked. At this stage Marcel had no idea, but he would do his best to find out. But because it was an undercover assignment it was not easy to extract information. All they could do was wait!

Several days had passed and no new information had been made available. Lan Mei and the girls were petrified at the thought of Zian having to swim ashore in the dark, not knowing anything about the area, or if there were sharks in the water. Neither he nor the girls had had any swimming lessons, so how was he going to reach the shore? Chen knew he had to get some information on the ship's whereabouts, then hopefully he could arrange for Zian and the others to be picked up by a motor launch, after having jumped overboard. But first he had to get the relevant information, and time was of the essence! Soon the fourteen days would be up, and the officials would come aboard to check for Covid.

The next news that came through was indeed grim. The father and his teenage son had died of Covid, leaving the wife and three children remaining on the ship alone. Now a new problem had arisen: the bodies would have to put overboard so as not to draw attention. This was devastating for the family members, but there was no other option. With risk came consequences! Chen felt sick for the wife and children, and he knew they had now become his problem and he could not abandon them; they would have to be rescued alongside Zian. "Imagine that poor mother, Chen, if she had to jump into the sea, how could she save three children? She must be terrified; we have to help her," pleaded Lan Mei. But until he got more information as to where the ship was anchored, they could do nothing.

Ten days had now passed, and time was running out, Chen couldn't make any arrangements; he was at a loose end. He didn't even know what port the ship was meant to berth at. Something had to happen fast. He prayed to the gods for an answer and answer they did! Marcel came back to Chen and supplied him with all the information he needed, so now he could start to make some progress. First, he had to catch a plane to a town nearest to the port, then he would arrange for a launch to go out to sea. He had been told the ship's captain would flash a light ten minutes before the passengers jumped overboard. This would give Chen and the launch crew time to come near to the ship and pick them out of the water. They did not want the ship's paying passengers to witness this event, so the captain's reputation would remain intact. He showed no mercy towards these people, although he had been paid handsomely. He had certainly not bargained on any complications along the way, but Covid had put paid to an otherwise uncomplicated delivery! He would think twice before putting himself in jeopardy again.

Chen and the launch crew saw the light flashing, so picked up speed and headed towards the ship. They could see the ship's outline and as they came near, they turned off the motor and sat in wait. There on the back deck, in the partial dark, stood figures. These must be the ones ready to jump. Chen knew he had to pick up five people, Zian and the remaining family members. Several minutes went by and they heard the first splash followed by several more. They turned the motor on and gently steered towards the splashes. The first person they pulled out was a child, then another and another. Where was the fourth and the mother? They circled around amid the cries of the children, who were looking for their mother. Where was Zian? He was still missing, but it was then Chen spotted the mother so they pulled her aboard. The family was safe, soaking wet and cold, but safe! But what of Zian? Everyone on board was looking for him. They went round and round in circles, and Chen was beside himself. Panic started setting in; where was he? He prayed that nothing had happened to him. He asked the family if they had seen him jump, but none of them could honestly say they had. Was he still on the ship? They spent another hour searching but to no avail. Now it was time to head back as the sea was starting to get angry. Chen was heartbroken and the tears flowed, followed by sobs. Had he failed?

The mother and her family were sympathetic towards Chen; he had rescued them but not Zian. "Perhaps he is still on the ship. He was petrified at the thought of jumping into the sea," said the mother. "Do you think that might be where he is?" asked Chen. "Yes, he said he couldn't swim, that he would drown, so he has probably decided at the last moment not to take the risk." This left Chen clinging to a smidgen of hope. How was he going to explain this to Lan Mei and the girls? Would they understand? One thing was for sure, he would not be going back without him. He would wait until the ship berthed. Now to ring Lan Mei at home and explain what had happened. "Oh Chen, that is so sad, but we must have faith, for all we have gone through, we will get results. I am happy the family are all together; are they going to be okay?" she asked. Chen had arranged to meet her the next morning when they were dry and warm and had had a good sleep. He himself was ready for bed. Chen's night was restless. He tossed and turned, and thoughts of Zian never left his mind. Where was he, was he safe, what would happen to him if he was still on the ship?

He was happy when dawn finally arrived. He was like a caged lion, raring to get on the trail and do something. He dressed and grabbed a quick bite then he was on his way to the port, where he would spend whatever time it took to find Zian. On his way he met the rescued family. They looked entirely different today, not like the drowned rats he pulled from the sea the previous night. "Thank you for rescuing us. God only knows what would have happened if we had been left to our own survival. I dread to think. I may have had to make choices, then I would never have been able to live with myself. We are indebted to you!" she said as she held out her hand to shake his. "I'm sorry you didn't find Zian, but we discussed it this morning; none of us saw him jump from the ship. We think he could still be on board, so perhaps he will have the sense to hide until the ship gets nearer the port." With this news Chen's hope was renewed. "Are you going to manage okay financially without your husband?" he asked. "We knew we were taking a risk, but we made a promise to each other that should anything happen to anyone, the rest had to remain as a family. We had to leave China immediately as my husband was a diseases expert and he had uncovered something unsavoury. He was about to make an announcement, but the authorities found out and were about to imprison our whole family. Financially we are okay, but thank you." Chen gave them his phone number in case anything went amiss in the future. It was time to say their final farewells as Chen was itching to get to the port.

Marcel had gone, his next mission was calling him, and he couldn't wait round as his time was of the essence; in other words, another rescue was awaiting him. Chen found a seat on the wharf where he could see every angle, waiting for however long it took for Zian's ship to arrive. He knew he would become bored; he wanted action, but patience was a virtue at this critical time. His mind switched to Zian: what must he be thinking, was he frightened? The poor boy must have panicked when he knew he had to abandon ship. So many thoughts were swirling around in Chen's mind; in fact the whole day passed before he realised that darkness was creeping in. This was only because an elderly man tapped him on the shoulder as he thought something had happened. This woke Chen up from a catnap. 'Oh well, back tomorrow, hopefully some action would be forthcoming?' he muttered to himself.

As Chen made his way down to the port the next morning, he was surprised to see a ship near to berthing. Was this the one Zian was on? He did not know the ship's name as it was dark two nights ago when he went to sea. His heart was pounding. Was he about to see Zian? The horn blasted as he made his way onto the wharf, and people were hurrying to be there for the ship's arrival. Chen stood and surveyed the deck where people were waiting to disembark. This was a freight ship, but it had paying passengers to help offset costs. Officials were setting up a table to test those coming ashore, making sure they didn't have a high temperature, as they handed over their passports. Chen went into panic mode wondering what would happen to Zian, as he thought he didn't have a passport. Suddenly his eyes were drawn to a small figure hanging over the side of the ship near where the lifeboats were attached; was he about to jump? He rushed closer. Yes, it was a young boy. Was this Zian?

Chen had to cause a distraction before the boy jumped, so he yelled, "Help, help some thieves have stollen my wallet. They went that way." The focus of the bystanders turned in the direction he was pointing. When he looked again the figure had disappeared. He ran to the side of the wharf and saw the boy floundering, barely able to keep his head above the water. He called to him, "Is that you, Zian? Swim over to the pier and hold on. I'll find a rope and throw it over the wharf for you to grab." With this he spotted an old mooring line lying on the wharf near an empty fish crate. He grabbed it and rushed back, then dropped the end over the wharf. He leaned over and yelled, "I'm Chen. Grab the rope and hold on tight, as soon as the coast is clear I'll pull you up. Stay strong young man!" There was no reply, but a tug on the rope let Chen know this was his response. He hoped the people would leave the wharf soon, as he didn't know how long Zian could hold onto the rope. It was getting cold and a breeze had come up, causing quite a swell around the piers. It was time to act. He started to pull up the rope, but it was not easy. How would he disguise Zian, once he had him ashore? Then he remembered the empty fish crate. He walked the rope along until he reached the crate; this would hide him from view. He kept pulling as he knew Zian's strength would wane very soon, so it was imperative to act fast. At last he saw a hand reaching over the wharf, he leaned forward and grabbed it. "Good man, Zian, hold on to me," then he was able to haul him on to the wharf. The young lad was shivering, his teeth were chattering and his lips were blue, while tears streamed down his face. Chen pulled Zian to him and held on tightly. "Thank God you are safe," he whispered. Suddenly Chen felt Zian's body go limp, and he slumped unconscious in his arms. Chen sobbed as he held onto this traumatised lad. He could feel the coldness that had engulfed him, so he took off his jacket and wrapped it around him. There they sat for the next hour, but now Chen had to get him somewhere warm.

Coming towards them were two fishermen dressed in their wet weather gear and their gumboots. He called to them, "Excuse me, my son fell off the wharf into the sea. He is suffering from shock. Can you help me get him to the cab-stand at the end of the wharf?" They were only too happy to help carry Zian to where he needed to go. "If you give us a minute, we will give you a lift home," they offered. Chen thought for a minute. This might be the best way to go, because if in the future things became complicated, there would be no back tracing through public transport. "Thanks, that would be great. We are staying at a motel," he replied. He didn't give the name of the motel, as there were four different ones next to each other; he would just get dropped off in the middle. By doing this there was no trace to which one they were staying in. Chen was very thorough in covering his steps; his past had made him this way … it was called survival!

Zian was starting to respond to the warmth from Chen's body as he cradled him in his arms. He looked into Chen's eyes and managed a weak smile. This tiny acknowledgement sent a warm feeling to Chen's heart. Already he felt love for this lonely soul; this was Tan's son, who had been entrusted to him through tragedy, but nonetheless he felt it was an honour and he would protect him to the end. Was this the son he secretly hoped for, but because of Lan Mei's sadness of not being able to provide him with children, it was a secret he kept to himself? He loved Lan Mei; she was his brave warrior, and she had been through so much and not once did she ever give up – she fought on!

Chen tucked Zian in his bed as he still hadn't recovered from the shock and he was too weak to stand in a hot shower. Besides he might feel embarrassed exposing his body to a complete stranger; Chen was sensitive on these matters. Zian closed his eyes and drifted off to sleep feeling safe and protected; the nightmare was over. Now it was time for Chen to let the rest of his family know what drama had been created within the last forty-eight hours. The girls would probably think it was excitement, but to Chen it was a life-or-death situation. Lan Mei couldn't help but sob when she heard the whole story, but to finally have the last family member was a blessing beyond belief. "What is he like, Chen?" she asked. "You wouldn't believe it; he is the spitting image of Tan. Oh, Lan Mei we are so lucky, we have now grown to a family of five. We will stay another night then we will fly home, I would like some time with him alone, as the girls will take over when they get back together. See you soon my love!"

Through the night Chen could hear Zian calling out, so he went and sat on his bed. He seemed a little delirious, and this bothered him. Did he have the virus, or was it the horror he had been through and was reliving? He stayed with him until he settled. Next morning when Chen arose and went to the kitchen there was Zian making some toast. "Good morning. How are you feeling today?" asked Chen. He looked at Chen and smiled, "Thank you for everything, I'm better today, I'm happy now that all the drama is over. You know I thought I would drown when we were told we had to jump overboard, as I can't swim," then the tears started. Chen asked him to come and sit with him on the settee where the two of them held on to each other. "I'm sorry," he sobbed, "I was so frightened, I thought I was going to die." "Nothing bad will ever happen to you again, I promise you that. I worked with your father at the laboratory, and one day I will tell you all I know. Do you remember him?" Chen asked. "No, I try to remember what he looked like, but his face has gone from my memory." Chen told him he just needed to look in the mirror, and he would see a younger version of his father. "Really!" he smiled.

The plane had just landed. Lan Mei and the girls were going to be there to greet them. Chen was so excited; his family was now complete. What would the girls' reaction be? Zian and Chen made their way to the terminal to meet the rest of the family. The building was nearly brought down by the screaming of the girls as they spotted their brother. "Zian, Zian," they yelled as they both ran into his arms. Tears flowed like a river, and cuddles were aplenty. "You will love living here Zian. We are so lucky. You should see where we live" … and on it went. Chen took Lan Mei's hand. Here was their ready-made family, a dream that had come to life!

●22

WHAT WOULD THE FUTURE HOLD?

A LOT HAD HAPPENED since the family were reunited. Sadness was mixed with joy. Chen had received a call from China, and on the line was the new lady who was administering the trust fund, as Lanying had passed away with the virus. The authorities had taken her away when it was apparent that she had something to do with the children's disappearance, but by this time she was very sick and didn't live very long. Their whereabouts was still being sought by Chinese authorities. Because Lanying had played an important part in all their lives, they dedicated a room to her in the house, where they would meet and pray every Sunday morning. She was never going to be forgotten.

Zian could not believe the new life he had joined, but he embraced it with excitement and disbelief. He, like the girls, found the Japanese custom of bowing to be funny at first, but soon took it on board to be an everyday occurrence. He went to the same school as the girls and enjoyed every moment. It was fun to be driven everywhere by their own driver and he, like Ling, loved the bonsai glasshouse. This was also his favourite place, when he wasn't in the office with Chen. They were the best of buddies.

Today Lan Mei received a phone call to see if she and Chen would do the final live talkshow, as people wanted to know how the trust fund was going and whether people were still needing financial help. Also, she was asked to speak on the subject of the virus and how it made young women sterile. She had learned a lot on this subject over the past year and was writing a thesis on 'To eradicate and depopulate'. This was a highly controversial subject, but it had to be put out there for the world to take on board. She told the host she and Chen would talk it over, as now they had a ready-made family, all from the tragedy of the virus. To the host, this sounded like a good story, but were Chen and Lan Mei willing to put their story out to the public, especially when it concerned the children? Perhaps the story could be made public, but no images would be allowed as this would be an invasion of their privacy! The children didn't need any more disruptions.

Both Chen and Lan Mei agreed to a final talkshow as they knew people in their home province in China were still in need of the trust funds. Still the Chinese authorities knew nothing about, or had anything to do with, the money, so it was going to the right destination and helping the disadvantaged whose lives were unfairly affected. The host wanted the children to be part of the interview, but Chen feared repercussions may follow, so the answer was no! They brought the children to Tokyo with them along with their driver and while the interview was on, the driver would take the children to go up in the lift to the top of the Tokyo Tower.

This interview was not as frightening as the first, as they knew the procedure. The host asked questions about their newly formed family, how the children came into their care, why they took them on, and the frightening situations they found themselves in to end up with them. Lan Mei tried to hold back her tears of joy as she told the host how they felt so gifted to have a ready-made family, especially as they were the children of people that had been part of their lives. They had also suffered through their ordeals, but now their lives were settled, they were loved and now they could just be themselves ... children. Chen told how the money was still helping those who needed it and he would be grateful if people continued donating. "How is the professor's work progressing under your care?" the host asked. "I am still carrying on with his work, although it was put on hold for several months, but now I am fully committed and following up on new leads, which will be put out there as they develop," replied Chen. "Lan Mei, can we get you back another day to talk us through your thesis on, 'Eradicate and depopulate'?" asked the host, to which she agreed.

Chen was still following the changing events of the virus. Just as it was thought to be under control, it had become more rampant in some countries, something happening much too often. In most of these countries big events were taking place and these were the ideal breeding grounds for the virus to spread. Highly populated countries where people lived in close proximity to each other were suffering the worst. The crucial element missing from many hospitals was a lack of oxygen. In India they only had enough oxygen to last a few more days, then people would be left to die, thus prompting a worldwide appeal, asking other countries for oxygen, and countries were responding. What country would be next? How long was this virus going to plague the universe?

With the Olympic games in July, Japan was clinging to the hope they would still go ahead, as they too saw an increase in virus cases. Chen and Lan Mei did wonder what joy the games would bring, with no crowds to cheer competitors on. Was this what the future was going to look like? Were people going to live more restricted lives? No-one could foresee, or even try to predict, what lay ahead.

Even with all the talk on vaccines, Chen was shocked to hear that a vaccinated person had in fact caught the virus. What did this mean for the future? Perhaps the vaccine was not the miracle cure as was first thought. Were the new variants untreatable at this stage, and was this the plan: to take out the elderly and the weak? Was this China's way to depopulate but keep young healthy brains alive? The professor's very words echoed in Chen's mind: 'Maybe this eradication was to replace World War 3, and instead of intelligent young lives being lost, just produce a virus and let it take out the elderly, as their lives were of less value. The cost of their healthcare had a huge impact on the local economy; the elderly took, whereas the young worked and contributed.'

Chen wondered if people had a choice ... a war ... or a virus, what might the outcome tell us?

ABOUT THE AUTHOR

Margaret Nyhon lives in Mosgiel, New Zealand, where she writes, paints and practises the crafts of printing and bookbinding.

She has worked extensively in hospitality management in New Zealand and resort management in Australia. The urge to trace her family history led her to the writing of her first non-fiction work, *de Marisco*. She has since written several fiction and non-fiction works. Margaret is married and has three adult children and two grandsons.

OTHER BOOKS BY THE AUTHOR

NON-FICTION

de Marisco

Freedom Knows No Boundaries

A Wake-up Call

A Shattered Dream Across the Tasman

Memories and Moving On

FICTION

Isobella (Book 1 in the *Isobella* series)

Isobella: Self Redemption (Book 2 in the *Isobella* series)

Papa's Girl Emmeline

Betrayal by an Irish Rose

Revenge for an English Lord (sequel to *Betrayal by an*

Irish Rose)

For Girls' Eyes Only

Daughters Lost to the Underworld

Pimchan and Amira